Also by William Freedman

Mighty Mighty
Age of Certainty (Editor)

LAND THAT I LOVE

WILLIAM FREEDMAN

Rebel ePublishers

Detroit   New York   London   Johannesburg

Rebel ePublishers
Detroit, Michigan 48223

Land That I Love
© 2010 by William Freedman

ISBN-13: 9780615939858
ISBN-10: 0615939856

Cover design by Mandie van der Merwe/*Love & Sweat*
Interior design by *Caryatid Design*

ACKNOWLEDGEMENTS

There are two characters in the book, Gene and Bertie, who are anachronistic representations of Gene Roddenberry and H.G. Wells, respectively. I express my debt to both these giants of speculative fiction.

For three generations, there has not been an American science fiction writer whose work has not been informed by Mr. Roddenberry's Star Trek milieu in all its incarnations, or who is unaware of such catch-phrases as "Beam me up!" As for Mr. Wells, strip away all other elements of the story, and the reader can confirm that the plot of this novel is a direct descendent of the plot of The War of the Worlds. Late in the book, Bertie quotes from that classic's uniquely styled narrator, and I am indebted to the original science fiction master for crafting that language.

The satirist's dilemma is to at once offend contemporaries who desperately need offending while showing the utmost respect to those who have come before. It is my hope, and that of the editors and the publishers of Land That I Love, that the estates of Messrs. Wells and Roddenberry accept all due apologies and consider this work to be an homage to our generation's shared cultural forebears.

Many thanks to Anna A. Volkova, Esq., for her sage counsel and, more so, for her abiding friendship.

I would also like to thank those who reviewed early drafts of the chapters which came together to form a novel. These include a host of participants in Charles Coleman Finlay's Online Writers Workshop, as well as classic-lineup members of LISciFi, the New York-based face-to-face critique circle: Wendy Delmater Thies, Eric Bresin, Amy Lau, Daniel

Braum, and Elizabeth Glover. Current members Ken Altabef, Kat Hankinson, Ben Parris and Miranda Suri provided invaluable support and encouragement during the publishing process, as have the scores of Facebook fans, Twitter followers and WordPress blog readers, many of whom are also long-standing friends or beloved family.

Finally, for their infinite patience and love, I thank and dedicate this book to my wife, Eileen, and our sons Eddie, James and John Liberty.

William Freedman,
11 March, 2010, West Hempstead, N.Y.

THE FLARE

The people of the sphere circling UV Ceti could sit at their terminals and work for a year straight. Their year was only seventeen hours long, but still.

All that industriousness came to an abrupt end when their sun surged. The red dwarf often flared, causing a bright, glowing haze on the synthesized planet's day side. But this time was different. Some had time to wonder if maybe the flare inhibitors were somehow knocked off-line. Some recluses on the night side had time to reflect on how much their loved ones, off-planet, would miss them.

But, ultimately, they were all consumed by the fireball. It wasn't instantaneous. Many had time to feel the searing heat, endure a wave of undiluted radiation poisoning and then experience exposure to pure vacuum as the atmosphere retreated with the sun.

Security cams were ubiquitous across all the Eminent Domain's worlds, so the rest of humanity, spread through scores of solar systems encompassing much of the galaxy's southern spiral, was able to witness the scene played out over and over from every angle. On screens throughout the Eminent Domain, paper flared and buildings melted. Men, women and children were reduced to ashen shadows on walls until a few moments later, when the walls themselves were reduced to ions. One sullen-faced man was seen to mouth the dying words, "But it was supposed to rain today."

Things like this didn't just happen. Artificial planets had been orbiting flare stars for generations and nothing like this had ever occurred. Something, or to be more precise, somebody, must have tampered with the processes that kept UV Ceti under human control.

The event took a name. Everybody knew where they were When All Hell Broke Loose.

THE CASE FOR WAR

President Sajak Pickfour was touring a clone farm when homeworlds policy advisor M. Griffin Croupier VII tugged at his sleeve. The president had his assistants hurriedly scroll up a primary-colored, ten-meter-long, construction-paper banner made by the artificial nine-year-olds spelling out, "WE LOVE AND TRUST YOU, MISTER PRESEDINT." Ten minutes later, Pickfour, Croupier and a small army of functionaries of all levels were strapped into the presidential interstellar transport, the Exceptional, and whisked into space.

Once it was determined that the transport was in no immediate danger, President Pickfour convened a meeting of those members of his Steering Committee who had been traveling with him.

"So ... what have you got for us, Lucky?" he asked, between crunches on an ice cube.

Croupier, a rail-thin man with a pencil-thin mustache, suppressed a grimace at the irritating sound and unwelcome nickname.

"Mister President," Croupier began, "UV Ceti flared and took out Habitat UV Ceti Alpha Zero Zero Eight."

"What's a Habit Alpha Double-Oh Eighty?" the president asked.

Croupier had been working for Pickfour for several months at that point and knew better than to be offended by his lack of attention. Croupier also understood that the president was using jargon when plain speech would do. Only the government called that satellite Habitat UV Ceti Alpha Zero Zero Eight. Everyone else called it by the ancient name used by the first settlers.

"MetLifeWorld," Croupier continued. "At least a quarter million Domestic citizens were lost – an uncounted number of foreign visitors as well – and there are people stranded on UV Ceti's outer planets, which can't support life for long without restraints on their sun's flaring activity."

"We got to find out who did this and deal with them," the president said.

"Do we even know that anyone did this as an act of aggression?" asked Claudia Thierstein, the president's foreign policy advisor, looking up from her note tablet.

"I mean, did anyone claim responsibility? We're just assuming it's sabotage, because we really don't have much to go on."

The president's cheek quivered and turned that particular shade of magenta it did when one of his trusted advisors questioned his assertions.

"The important thing now," Croupier continued, "is to rescue the people on the outer planets, tighten security around solar flare inhibitors throughout the Eminent Domain and make arrangements for the families of the MetLifeWorld vic ..."

He didn't get a chance to continue. An intern rushed in and panted out that a similar disruption had unleashed a neighboring sun, Luyten 726-8 A, on its own artificial planet. HomeDepotWorld was no more. And nobody, not Croupier, not Thierstein, thought for one second that it was a coincidence.

"I was right," the president said. "Now does anyone have

any idea who's capable of such evilness?"

"Well, if I had to pick someone," Thierstein said, trying to salvage her end of this discussion, "I'd say The Popular Front for the Defense of the Honor of Mother Earth."

"What's the Popular Honor of Defending the Front of ... What's that?" the president asked.

"It's a revolutionary organization that demands the entire populated galaxy be brought back under the authority of Earth, the origin planet," she replied.

"Oh, yes," the president said, nodding. "The Terrahists."

"Exactly, Mister President," Thierstein said, her mop of frosted hair bobbing with more vigor than her chin.

"Guess we just gotta go invade America," the president said.

"Sir," Croupier interjected, "although the Mother Earth movement is active in America and elsewhere on that planet, there's no reason to assume that the Americans are involved."

"Come again?" the president said, distracted by a piece of upholstery that was becoming detached from the arm of his chair.

"Well, the Terrahists are fanatics bent on bringing the entire galaxy under Earth control," Croupier explained, adding animated hand gestures and wild variations in the tone of his voice in order to capture some of his leader's attention. "The Americans are just a second-rate power looking to extend their regional hegemony. Any connection between ..."

"What I want to know," the president interrupted, "is how the Americans are involved."

"Well ... we can't be certain they are," Croupier continued.

"How do you mean?" the president asked.

"Maybe if we show this on a map?" Thierstein suggested.

Croupier projected a two-dimensional rendering of Earth's

surface for everyone's convenience.

"Earth hasn't had a functioning planetary government for some time," Croupier said. "As you can see, it's divided into a dozen regional blocs. Sometimes they cooperate - mostly they don't - and sometimes they wage active warfare against each other. The only thing they have in common is that the stateless Mother Earth movement functions throughout all their borders."

"So where's America?" the president asked. "Is it that big thingy at the bottom?"

"No, Mister President. It's in the western hemisphere," Thierstein said, then paused for the leader to catch up. After a couple of breaths, she felt compelled to say, "That's the one on the left." She observed the track of the president's eyes and was again compelled to comment, "No, Sir, the other left."

"Heidi, find out whose job it was to give me my dyslexia meds this morning and have him shot into space," the president directed an aide. Before she could proceed, he added, "and find out who was supposed to give me my memory enhancement tab, so I could remember to take it myself, then shoot him into space, too. We got to maintain a culture of accountability around here."

He shot his as-you-were-saying look at Thierstein.

"Although America is now ruled by the most brutal regime in its history, there's no clear link between it and the Terrahists," she summed up.

"Then how are the Americans involved?"

"They're not!" Thierstein said, louder than she intended, her patience exhausted. "There's nothing to suggest so, at least. Maybe they're involved. Probably they're not. There are Terrahists. There are Americans. Some Americans are Terrahists. Not all Terrahists are Americans."

"Sounds awful wishy-washy to me," the president said.

When Heidi came back in, the president directed her to

shoot Thierstein into space.

"Lucky," the president said, with a hand on Croupier's shoulder, "you're no longer my homeworlds advisor. You're my foreigners advisor. Now tell me what you think we should do to the Americans."

☆☆☆

Watts Barber, America's president, would concede to his critics – if any had still been alive – that he was born to few advantages and manifested fewer natural abilities as he matured. There was one thing he could do, however – better than anyone else in America – the one trait Americans revered above all else.

He could put a big ball through a small hoop.

In America that, combined with bottomless ambition and ruthlessness, was enough to propel someone to a life of wealth, prestige and political ascendancy. His playing days far behind him, Barber was still a tall, muscular, imposing figure with a shaven, sharp-angled head. And now that he didn't have to suit up for athletic competition, he could – and did – carry his old-style .38 all the time. His willingness to use it, together with his legendary aim, ensured that he would rise to the highest office in the land and stay there.

Barber sat on his throne as a courtier delivered his morning briefing.

"Your Presidential Highness, the ambassador from Florida wishes to sue for peace. His people ..."

"Gas 'em," the president said, as he munched a hamburger out of a foil wrapper.

"Yes, Sir. Also, the Religious Movement begs to discuss the possibility of not having your image displayed in such prominent fashion in all their ..."

"Gas 'em."

"Already took the liberty, Sir. The leader of the Minnesotan separatist movement wishes to settle differences amicably, without any further loss of life. They challenge you to a contest."

"Three-on-three?"

"Six-on-six."

"Never heard of that."

"Hockey."

"Nuke 'em. Anything else, Arsenio?"

"Just one thing, Sir. The Eminent Domain thinks we were behind When All Hell Broke Loose.

"Were we?"

"No, Sir."

"Oh," the president said, with a pensive inflection, which even his closest loyalists seldom heard. "Why not?"

☆☆☆

On a small, rustic, backwater planet known as EZPassWorld, deep in the far recesses of the Fifty-five Cancri system, a man sat cross-legged at the entrance to a shallow cave. His back was to a campfire that flared through the darkness almost to the edge of space, fed as it was by a low-gravity but oxygen-enriched atmosphere. *Let the arrogant ones find me*, he dared, *my task is completed.*

The man's face – lined but hairless – and chest – powerful and also hairless – were hunched over a small comnet transceiver. The transceiver itself was a masterwork of ingenuity, pieced together from the spare parts of a dozen predecessors.

"Come in, Mother Earth," he spoke into the transceiver. His voice was grave, deep and monotone, projecting calm despite the weight of too many concerns. "Acknowledge, please."

"We read you, Fifty-five Cancri," returned a tinny reproduction of a calm and careworn voice. The low fidelity didn't diminish a soothing tone that promised the comfort of a maternal embrace. The voice could have been that of Gaia, the origin world herself. "We have heard of your success. All Earth's hearts beat with yours this day. Your mission is accomplished. You and your party may now return home."

"I must return home alone," the man on the planetoid said. He almost let the sadness of losing his entire contingent creep into his voice.

"Our grandchildren's grandchildren will remember their names and honor them as heroes," the voice from Earth said, the speaker allowing herself the luxury of a tone that could convey empathy to her bereaved colleague. "They will also remember your name, Shoots at the Stars."

"You too shall be remembered by all who love Mother Earth, Fire from the Lake," the man said, shedding a single tear.

☆☆☆

Croupier wasn't happy about his demotion. In any other era, or in any other sovereign government, Claudia Thierstein's bad luck would have been to his good. But under President Sajak Pickfour of the Eminent Domain, foreign relations would always take a back seat to homeworlds policy. This struck Croupier as awfully shortsighted but, ultimately, he respected the unique perspective of the president. After all, foreigners couldn't vote for his re-election.

Croupier was stuck aboard the Exceptional for the better part of a week, before he was even permitted to phone home to say he was safe. He spent most of that time running simulations of possible outcomes of a strike against America. None of them resulted in the Eminent Domain dissolving into five hundred feuding solar systems or being overrun by the Kleptocosm, but none of them resulted in absolute success either.

As soon as he was permitted, he opened a secure link.

"Honey? ... Hey, me too. Sorry I couldn't call you till just now. It's a different galaxy today but at least we're both safe. That's the important thing ... I'm with the SteerCo now, babe, and we'll be going into a meeting in just a couple ... I love you too. But listen, I got some news and we'll talk about it in person. I'll be landing at Spaceport Trebek at 2660. Meet me ... You do the same. Gotta go. Love you. Bye."

A half dozen people were in the conference room when Croupier hustled in and found a seat. Croupier, the only career civil servant among them, took out his note tablet, scribbled the date in the left margin of the top sheet, paged through assorted briefing documents in an effort to look busy. Then he realized: He was the highest-ranking advisor in the room.

"So what have we got for the president?" he asked, as he poured himself some water.

"We have an array of military options," said a squinting Admiral Reit Daytrader, as his assistant handed out printed copies of the military chief's latest spreadsheet. "There's a different technical procedure for targeting a stable yellow star, rather than a red dwarf but ... we could explode their sun. Or we could use high-atmosphere nuclear explosions to cause an extinction event on the planet itself. Or we could use a ground assault that could occupy either America or the entire land mass. How much do you want to spend?"

"It's not a matter of expense," Croupier responded, glancing over his copy of the spreadsheet. "None of these options furthers our foreign policy."

"Mister Croupier is right, Admiral," said Ambassador Ziglar Tobaccoflack in his crystalline tenor voice, blue eyes twinkling over high cheekbones. "Right now, every civilization in the Grand Organ supports anything we would do to attack the Terrahists, although they won't have the stomach for blowing up their sun because there are other inhabited planets in that system."

"Even if we extinguished life just on Earth, the Grand Organ wouldn't go along," Croupier said, nodding along with the high-ranking, high-profile diplomat. "And we can't direct space-based weapons against America, without some drift into Earth's other nations and collateral damage on even that small a scale, still won't sit well with our allies."

"How very inconvenient. Why is that?" the ambassador asked. His permanent theatrical smile and unwrinkled brow belied the upward inflection in his voice.

"Raw materials," Croupier replied, holding up Admiral Daytrader's handout as a literal example. "America is the galaxy's largest source of dumb-paper. The whole country's overgrown with trees."

"Not to mention," said Brosius Slipfall, the president's trade advisor, "we import a lot of paper from America ourselves. Our economy would grind to a halt if we were to destroy that key trading partner."

"So you're recommending we find a more peaceful settlement?" Croupier asked.

"No," Slipfall replied, "I'm recommending we go in there and take it over."

"Admiral," Croupier addressed Daytrader, "what kinds of resources will you need to capture and secure America?"

"Two million, three million troops at most," the admiral said, scratching at his thinning hair. "Budget for four."

He then took out a calculator and started pushing buttons – the zero most of all – as his eyes, usually squeezed into a squint, bulged.

☆☆☆

Events were about to overtake the planned invasion of America, though.

Sanmateo Veecey could have directed his life along any number of routes. He was by all accounts bright, cultured, warm-hearted and born into one of the Eminent Domain's most respectable families. He could have been known as Pastor Veecey or Professor Veecey or Doctor Veecey. One thing he wasn't, though, was self-directed. So after the Academy the feckless graduate stayed in the army, for a bit longer than he expected to, as he mulled over what kind of vocation he'd really like to pursue.

Some years later, Major General Veecey found himself in command of Domestic troops in the Hyades cluster When All Hell Broke Loose. It was not a glamorous assignment. Most of the Hyades worlds were hostile to the Eminent Domain, for reasons unfathomable to Veecey's fellow Domestic citizens. But nobody back home worried too much about the ragtag, backwater Hyades gangs. They were too small, too divided, too weak and too diffuse in their anger against other leading Grand Organ members to be considered a threat.

Still, Veecey, the highest ranking officer of either gender or of any spacefaring military who wore a ponytail, was only surprised and not really shocked when comnet chatter throughout the cluster spiked immediately after When All Hell Broke Loose.

In the immediate aftermath, Veecey and his entire command-and-control staff crowded the flagship's intel room 'round the clock. Every chirp and twitter was translated, analyzed, classified, reviewed and, ultimately, discarded. It was a long, arduous task that was not in the least rewarding to anyone in the room.

Watch by watch, the intel room crowd thinned. Instead of there being twelve people trying to fit into a two-person room, there were eight. Soon it was down to five. Then it settled down to two. Then came the watch when Veecey was one of those two.

"Sir, I think we found our bad guys!" called out the electronically-altered voice of Lieutenant Iman Appdev, the young woman seated in front of him. A beautiful body was easy enough to come by in the Eminent Domain, where cosmetic surgery and gene therapy were performed on a walk-in basis. Even so, Appdev stood out. Any man alive would have been captivated by the bone structure of her ankles, the dimples in her elbows when she crossed her arms, the perfect symmetry of her scapulae, the exact shade of chestnut brown of her hair, so beyond mortal ken that Prometheus must have stolen it from Olympus and plea-bargained down to stealing fire. Appdev was so transcendently attractive that she didn't really need a face. This was fortunate, as she had the intel officer's prosthetic implants clogging every sensory organ, her voice synthesized out of a plate attached to her throat. Most days, she reset the voice plate before she went on shift so it would project a no-nonsense, get-the-job-done, professional military tone. In her haste to start that watch, though, she hadn't noticed that the voice plate was set to 'coo.'

"Can you translate the content?" the general asked.

"The signals seem to center on the Fifty-five Cancri system," the voice plate lilted in response.

"Yes, but what are they saying?"

"That it's a binary system with one yellow sun, which in turn, supports several terrestrial planets."

"Yes, I know, Lieutenant. Are there any language barriers we need to ..."

"One of those planets, EZPassWorld, has been on our watch list for some time."

"You can't hear a word I'm saying, can you?" the general observed.

"EZPassWorld has been under the rule of the Popular Front for the Defense of the Honor of Mother Earth for years."

"I've always found you very attractive."

"This de facto rule is not recognized by the Grand Organ or any of its members."

"You can't imagine how hard it's been working in close quarters with you like this when all I want to do is strap you to a bulkhead and make zero-gee love to you."

"The government-in-exile has a longstanding mutual

defense pact with the Eminent Domain, on which we have
not yet demonstrated the political will to act."

"You'd wake up to the aroma of the home-grown tea I'd
brew for you."

"But right now, we've got two bandits – one on a close-in
planetoid and another, judging from the trajectory of the
repeaters, somewhere on or close to Earth – bragging about
their roles in When All Hell Broke Loose. And we know that
the Mother Earth movement's troop strength is concentrated
in the governmental capital, the holy city and eight known
training camps. Surgical nuclear strikes would solve all our
problems in seconds. No member of the Grand Organ would
say we were doing anything other than defending ourselves
against further attacks."

"I know I'm old enough to be your father, but I'm OK
with that if you are. Oh, if only I weren't your commanding
officer! If only I could say all this when you could actually
hear me! I'd whisk you away to a life of love and luxury on
a warm planetoid twenty light-years from the nearest civilized
world. It's been in my family for generations. We grow roses
and hyacinths and lavender there. It's breathtaking when
you first see it from space ... the whole atmosphere is
scented like the sweetest perfume."

"What's that about perfume, Sir?" the junior officer said
in her natural voice, as she disconnected her face – which
was just pretty, not stunning, because she didn't see the
point in spending money on the one part of her body that
was rarely seen – from the intel grid. She then rinsed the
adhesive out of her mouth and gargled.

"Huh?" the general said, his face for the moment
contorted into the mask of a teenage boy caught sneaking
back in after curfew. "You must've heard wrong, Lieutenant.
Not your fault ... I guess I have a strong regional accent. I
was just complimenting you on how efficiently you perfume
your duties."

He stared at her as she massaged her forehead, eyelids, ears and cheeks. Intel officers always did this after several hours under the prosthetics. There was nothing erotic about it, except to Veecey. He resisted the urge to offer to help.

"Have the coordinates of the Terrahist strongholds replicated over to Guidance, asap," he said instead.

"Yessir."

Veecey invoked a time-honored foundation of the Eminent Domain's foreign policy, in which senior military officers in remote expanses of space could, on their own initiative, take action against known hostile combatants or interstellar criminals without waiting for authorization from back home. If the action proved to be justified, the officer would be commended. If it turned out to be unjustified, it would be assumed that the officer acted with the best intentions, in the best interests of the homeworlds, based on the best information available. There would be no repercussions.

This was known as the Oops Doctrine.

Within the hour, a total of 28 megatons of enriched Oops fell on EZPassWorld, enough to wipe out all vestiges of Terrahist domination without harming most of the indigenous, rural civilian population.

The people of EZPassWorld were freed from Terrahist tyranny, accepted the collateral damage as inevitable, and thanked the Eminent Domain for their deliverance. Soon, the local citizens were able to settle back into their pre-Terrahist routines and return to pursuing their unique, time-honored customs: blood feuding, drug dealing and bestiality.

☆☆☆

As soon as his small craft left EZPassWorld's atmosphere, Shoots at the Stars saw the massive Domestic flotilla. He saw them launch their warheads. At first he figured they were firing on his position, but the missiles sailed past on all sides. Clearly, the sky soldiers were targeting the planet below.

He realized in an instant: They were serious this time. They were going to reduce the planet to rubble, if need be, to avenge his actions.

Typical Eminent Domain maneuver, Shoots at the Stars thought, letting out a heavy sigh. They were after him, whether or not they even knew who he was. In either event, they were decimating a planet because he had been there.

Despite wearing a UV-visored helmet, covering all portholes with blast shielding, pressing his face flat against an interior bulkhead and closing his eyes as tight as he could, Shoots at the Stars was blinded for a moment by the explosions on the trembling world, a mere 200,000 kilometers off his aft sensor array.

☆☆☆

Veecey reported the victory, via a secure comnet channel, directly to President Pickfour's selection to head the Eminent Domain's military, Admiral Reit Daytrader.

Daytrader's appointment to the Steering Committee had surprised no one. He did, on his own merit, have a successful military career. Starting out as a humble procurement officer, he rose through the middle ranks, then the senior ranks and then to the highest position to which an officer in his specialization could aspire: Accountant General. In his time, Reit Daytrader had done it all: covert accounts receivable, posting to ledger under enemy fire and, most daring of all, the midnight pension raid on IBMWorld.

Combine that with his family's defense-industry wealth – much of it invested in the "Pickfour for President" campaign – and there were no other serious contenders. None that weren't closely related, at any rate. A significant proportion of the officer corps attended the family reunion he hosted every year.

"Oh, bad luck," Admiral Daytrader told Croupier at the next day's strategy session which, for the first time in many days, was held at the presidential palace, in the normal gravity of the Eminent Domain's capital world. A translucent green visor shaded his squinting eyes. "The Terrahists responsible for When All Hell Broke Loose have been identified, tracked, targeted and destroyed."

"How's that bad?" Croupier asked, filling his glass to the brim with iced water.

"It means there's no link to America," the admiral responded.

"So? We just call off the invasion."

"Mister Croupier, I must beg to disagree. All it means is that we have to think of another reason to invade America," the admiral corrected. "You really haven't been on President Pickfour's foreign policy team long, have you, son?"

"No, but I'm a fast learner," Croupier said, smoothing his pencil-thin moustache. "So I need to know two things. One: what justification should Tobaccoflack offer to the Grand Organ for the invasion? Two: what's the real reason?"

☆☆☆

"WTF?!" President Pickfour inquired, more angry than any of the advisors in the Steering Committee meeting expected.

"Yes, Sir," Croupier replied.

"What do you mean by that?"

"Weapons of Tremendous Force."

"Oh, that's different," the president said. "Where I come from it stands for something else."

"We have good intelligence that the American government has been developing these weapons, against Grand Organ sanction, for some time," Croupier explained.

"What kind of weapons?" the president asked.

"Terrible ones, Mister President," Admiral Daytrader answered. "They have the most awful weapons in the known galaxy - weapons that could only have been conceived in the most warped, hateful, evil minds ever to plague humanity. But don't worry, Sir, ours are even better."

"I think what the admiral is saying," Croupier continued,

regaining the floor, "is that we should put forward the search for WTFs as a reason for a pre-emptive strike against America, in order to enable us to conduct it under Grand Organ auspices."

"Tell me again, why do we have to do that?" the president asked. "Here in the Eminent Domain, we have a long history of going it alone when need be."

"Well, the political capital we received When All Hell Broke Loose would be squandered, if we were to ignore the will of the Grand Organ," Croupier said.

"Besides, why not get Associated Market troops in there as well?" Admiral Daytrader added. "That way we get Market governments to buy Domestic ordnance with their strong currency, swap it back when exchange rates correct and ... we could actually pull off this invasion below cost. Oh, and maybe save some lives."

☆☆☆

The American president decided late one afternoon to go out to the driving range and hit a bucket of balls. That those lacquered balls had been surgically removed from political prisoners was a source of amusement to Watts Barber. Arsenio, his body man, placed one on the tee, then watched as his leader hit it three hundred yards, straight as a laser.

"Great shot, Sir," Arsenio said, the president's golf bag strapped to one arm, the paper sack containing the remnants of the president's late lunch clutched under the other. "But please try to make this bucket last for a while. We're running low on balls."

"Why's that?"

"Running low on political prisoners."

"If you're going to have a problem," Barber philosophized, as he teed one up himself, "that's a great problem to have. Fore!"

Three-twenty-five, that time.

"The news isn't all good, though, Sir."

"Out with it, Arsenio," the president said, wiping the sweat off his shaven brow. "You think I'd shoot you in the eye just for being real with me?"

"No, Sir," Arsenio lied. "I've just been trying to find the right time, the right words...."

"Spill it," Barber said. He leaned on his Big Bertha and focused full attention on his aide.

"The Eminent Domain is on the brink of declaring war."

"They've been talking that kind of smack since Pickfour took over. What's different this time?"

"They're going to the Grand Organ, making a big production about how we ... uh ... you ... must be stopped."

"And you think Pickfour's going to send millions of troops dozens of light-years just to cap me?"

"It's not like you two don't have history, Sir."

"Yeah, that's right, we got history," Barber said, as his gaze wandered from the precise centers of Arsenio's pupils, to a point somewhere over the horizon. Arsenio knew that look. Barber's gaze skidded up the neglected river of tar, once known as Interstate 15, toward the abandoned campus of the University of Nevada at Las Vegas. He remembered the first time he'd called Las Vegas home: his sixteen-week college career. Had that worked out otherwise, he wouldn't have amassed so much power but, no doubt, he'd have been more content. Nostalgia for those long-gone days – and resentment toward the idiot who had precipitated their end – faded. "But this is business. Payback's great as long as it's free, otherwise it ain't worth it."

"With all due respect, Your Presidential Highness, this Pickfour is not as enlightened as you."

"True, true," the president said as he teed up another ball, settled into his stance and contemplated the point at which tee, ball and club would soon all intersect. "Guess it couldn't hurt to put our contingency plans into place. Set it up. Send Dishy underground to set up an insurgency command. Get

Emelem in here - we got to sit down. See to it that the Catalina's fully stocked. Book me the usual rooms."

"Yes, Sir," Arsenio said. Relieved that this conversation had gone as well as it had, he turned on his heel to get off the range before the conversation could take another turn.

"And Arsenio!" the president called after him. The body man decided not to pretend he was out of earshot because he was, after all, still within pistol shot. "Bring me another bucket of balls. It's getting dark, so make it the glow-in-the-dark ones. From Minnesota. Fore!"

☆☆☆

The Hall of All Opinions, the chamber that housed the broadest array of representatives to the Grand Organ, bustled with last-minute activity. Functionaries came and went, handing documents and paper cups to the heads of missions, or taking documents and paper cups away. A cacophony of journalists yammered into galacticam lenses along the perimeter. An impromptu hush came over the hall as the lights dimmed.

"Distinguished delegates," the sergeant-at-arms called out over a public address system, "the ambassador plenipoten-tiary from the Eminent Domain, His Excellency Ziglar Tobaccoflack."

Total darkness enveloped the dais until a pin spot illuminated Tobaccoflack's face. Makeup accentuated his high cheekbones and drew attention to his sparkling blue eyes. His hair, dyed jet black, was slicked back with a part down the middle. The spotlight reflected off his dazzling white teeth, back into the assembly's eyes. "My people called on me because I'm the pro ... at explaining why we need to go ... into battle on Earth *mundo*," he began, fingers snapping, as an arpeggio tinkled around high C on a piano somewhere. "It's really important and you should know ... So. Let's. Put. On. A. Sh-o-o-o-o-o-o-w!"

The stage lights came up, revealing Tobaccoflack in all his

PREPARATIONS

Somewhere in America, a young man was walking down the street, his gait casual and confident, despite tightly pressed buttocks. Tall, sandy-haired, high-cheekboned, broad-shouldered, he wasn't just American; he was what used to be called 'all-American.' Dressed in casual, elegant layers of brown and tan, he scratched at the half-week's stubble on his cheeks as he ambled along a downtown street.

His name was G.Q. Celltower.

As he passed a dollar store someone, with an earpiece curled under a sweatshirt hood, barreled out of the doorway and took Celltower's legs out from under him.

The sandy-haired man reached for the 9mm pistol stashed in his jacket pocket, but too late. Another assailant jumped out of the doorway of a dollar store farther up the block and, still at a run, kicked Celltower in the chest, sending the pistol skidding across the street, where it was picked up by another member of the shadowy unit, who was loitering in front of a dollar store there. Celltower, already knocked to his knees, tumbled backward. Two others, whom he realized had been following him since he passed a dollar store a block back, came running up to him as he lay splayed out on the sidewalk, flat on his back. They drew rifles on him, poking the muzzles straight into the flesh under his jaw and left armpit.

The one in the hooded sweatshirt pressed his pistol against one of those high, stubbly cheeks.

His name was Chuck-Claude Spamblocker and he had known Celltower since grade school.

"You owe us a beer," Spamblocker said.

☆☆☆

Two of the highest ranking members of President Sajak Pickfour's Steering Committee sat in a plush office in the presidential palace, sipping icy spring water drawn from a tap in the mahogany paneled wall, wadding up unused tablets of paper and shooting them at - or at least in the general direction of - the trash can.

The decision on whether to invade America had to be made that week - because the invasion was scheduled for the week following - and there were still many important details to sort out. Not the least of them was the choice of commanders.

"So who are you going to get?" Ambassador Ziglar Tobaccoflack, the guest, asked his old friend Admiral Reit Daytrader, whose office this was.

"Still trying to figure that one out, Zig," Daytrader said, as he took squinty aim, banked one off the paper roll of his antique adding machine, watched it carom off the far wall, drop onto the rim of the trash can for an agonizing second, then fall to the carpet. His face scrunched up into the equivalent of an obscenity.

"Know who I'd feature?" the ever-composed, often flamboyant diplomat asked, throwing his wad of paper to a point somewhere in the same gravity well as the trash can.

"Can't say that I do," Daytrader responded, declining to clarify whether or not he cared.

"Veecey."

The game stopped. From under his emblematic green eyeshade, Daytrader glared at Tobaccoflack's presumption.

"How do you do that?" the admiral asked.

"Do what?" Tobaccoflack countered, leaning back in his

seat, arms stretched over his head as he took – and missed – another shot, his classic wingtip shoes resting on his host's desk.

Daytrader rose to his feet, leaned forward over his desk and made wild gestures with his hands.

"That. You're splayed out like you're going to roll over and go to sleep. You're going to leave shoe polish stains on an oaken desk I couldn't afford if I had to pay for it. Then you rile me by trying to tell me how to do my job. And I just know you're going to walk out of this office in a couple of minutes, be accidentally-on-purpose buttonholed by the press, hold an impromptu news conference about something you don't know anything about, come across like an expert in everything ... and you'll look good doing it ... not a hair out of place, not a scuff on your shoes no matter how much damage they do to my desk ... not even a wrinkle in your suit. How do you do that?"

"It's what I do," Tobaccoflack said, with a shrug that conveyed the exact blend of modesty and insouciance he intended.

Daytrader sat back down and, with a roll of his eyes, asked, "Why Veecey?"

"Well, why not?"

"He's just not a war fighter," Daytrader said.

"Neither are you. You're an accountant."

"Which is why I'm not leading the action. I'm just here to make sure it comes in under budget. I need someone with leadership experience and operational skills in that job."

"But look at what he did in the Hyades cluster."

"After a career made out of showing up on time and keeping out of trouble, he got lucky. He was stationed there because it was of no strategic importance."

"The only reason Veecey hasn't made more of a splash up to now is that at heart he's a modest guy. I looked up his Academy record. He was top in his class."

"Of course he was top in his class," said Daytrader,

steaming at the impudence. "He majored in music history."

"Still, he made the decision to stick with the military. A lot of cadets end up putting in their minimum time, then go do something else with their lives."

"You know why he stayed in the military?" Daytrader countered. "We have bands! He hung around the first fifteen years because we offered the only full-time job in this spiral of the galaxy for a clarinet player. We didn't put him into line functions until he outranked all the conductors."

After much deliberation, Admiral Reit Daytrader made the most important decision in his career, choosing Sanmateo Veecey to command the American theater of operations, because it was the fastest path to getting Tobaccoflack out of his office.

☆☆☆

The new foreign policy advisor took a stroll along commons that rolled lengthwise between the Avenue of Edicts and the Avenue of Executive Fiat.

M. Griffin Croupier VII always enjoyed long walks through that park where verdant, manicured lawns were dotted at respectable distances with somber statuary, renowned museums and overpriced merchandise stands. Walking through the commons, one could see the monuments to the whole glorious history of the Eminent Domain:

• The nasty Rebellion in which captured Terran occupation troops were subjected to alternating high atmosphere and ground level pressure, until they exploded in clumps of flesh, bone and blood bubbling with nitrogen.

• The fratricidal Internal Matter, a long and vicious draw that ended with the compromise that clones, technically, would be freed from their legal status of property but would have no actual rights.

• The War That Had to Be Fought Twice, in which the Eminent Domain and its allies endured a horrible conflict, accepted the unconditional capitulation of the forces of the Associated Market, then had to fight the same war over again a generation later, when the losers found out that the instrument of surrender had never been notarized.

History didn't concern Croupier at the moment, though. He was just a man walking through the park, hand in hand with the love of his life. He turned to steal a kiss – an uncharacteristic public display of full, unabashed affection that could almost have set his moustache on fire.

"Mmm, that was nice, Griff."

"For me too, Steve."

"Occasion?"

"No, you're irresistible every day."

Croupier's husband blushed.

"Honestly, the occasion is I've been so busy justifying the invasion that I hardly get to see you," Croupier said, as he locked eyes with Steve so intently he almost tripped over a fire hydrant.

"So it's on," Steve said, then read Croupier's face. "I didn't hear it from you, luv. I just hope it's all over quickly. You can't keep this up forever."

"No, but I have to, for now. You knew this when you married me, honey. I'm bound by duty."

"To the Domain, sure, I get that. But does that Pickfour character really deserve this level of dedication?"

"The Domestic people think so and I'm not going to argue with them."

"But he's so ... so ..." Steve struggled to find the right word, then gave up, "... dumb."

"I used to think so."

"You don't anymore?"

"Well he's certainly distracted," Croupier mused. "And he lacks any curiosity about things that don't interest him. He doesn't take advice well. Or criticism at all. I haven't detected anything in him that resembles analytical skills, or any kind of methodical reasoning."

"So he's dumb."

"Yeah, you win. He's dumb," Croupier conceded. "And that wouldn't be so bad."

"But?"

"But it's amazing how often he's right."

Admiral Reit Daytrader was still in his office late into the evening. Eyes squinting under his green eyeshade, he touched the panels on twelve different screens, each providing a different view of the Eminent Domain's military deployment: cash flow, accrual, economic value-added, market capitalization and so on. His scans were becoming more random and less constructive as time went on, so he decided it was almost time to call it a night.

As the lights up and down the corridor past his office went out, the antique gooseneck lamp on his desk highlighted his last read of a long day.

Musing over stray thoughts of retirement, Daytrader thumbed through the thick manila file labeled VEECEY, S. with three gold star stickers – the third affixed earlier that week.

Promotions on schedule ... a list of campaign ribbons, even if there were no decorations for conspicuous valor ... high performance and morale in units under his command ... exemplary conduct ... superior physical specimen for a man well into middle age.

No children ... never married ... never united. That seemed odd.

Results of the Lane-Broderick test suggested he was heterosexual.

Girlfriends? Nothing documented, so nothing long-term. *Even been laid? Come on,* Daytrader reasoned, *Veecey is a soldier. And a musician. And has great hair,* the rapidly balding Daytrader noted with envy.

On the highest floor of his towering residence, Watts Barber stood staring out at his view of the sunset. In the mornings it was his habit to wake up a little before dawn, then stroll from his bedroom to his private office and watch the sunrise over the capital's skyline. He was well aware this was probably his last sunset from that perch and that the morning would bring the last sunrise. He loved those three-sixty degree views. He knew he was going to miss them.

In the glass, he saw the spectral reflection of Arsenio, his body man, pulling clothes out of the wardrobe closet, folding them in perfect thirds and packing them in cases. Barber then heard the swish of elevator doors opening and heard a familiar voice.

"Watts, baby!"

It was Emelem Cox-Arquette, the one-time theatrical agent who, upon hearing about a tough-as-nails eighth-grader out of the roughest part of the 'burbs who couldn't miss from three-point range, suddenly changed careers and became a sports agent. Cox-Arquette, a chubby but oddly charismatic sort, became a father figure to the young athlete and, when the games were over and the endorsements dried up, was instrumental in helping Watts Barber's transition into his second career as a despot.

"Uncle!" Watts Barber exclaimed, pronouncing it more like 'onkl,' in flattering imitation of Cox-Arquette's Hollywoodese accent.

The two men embraced and Cox-Arquette kissed Barber's shaven pate. Arsenio caught himself rolling his eyes.

"What's the big production? You moving?" Cox-Arquette asked, gesturing to Arsenio, who was keeping his eyes to himself.

"Going underground, Uncle," Barber replied, leading the older, heavy-set man over to a couch. "Pickfour's boys are coming for me."

"It's not like you to run from a fight."

"It's like me to win. However I can."

"You want I should do something?"

"Yeah," Barber replied. "Wait 'til I'm gone. Then head out to the coast. Set up the operation out there. Keep Dishy on a leash. She'll be at our contingency base in Palm Springs."

"I should run the whole shebang?"

"Just till things blow over," Barber explained. "These space monkeys, they got no attention span. Once the money runs out, once the body count crosses some line, once the news gets old and they feel like changing the channel, they'll find a new hobby."

"Sounds like us, once upon a time."

"Comes around, goes around," Barber replied, as they shared a secret handshake and an even more secret smile. After a moment, Barber continued, "You should get going."

"Watch your back," Cox-Arquette said.

"One more cheeseburger and you probably could," Barber kidded.

A swish of the elevator doors and Cox-Arquette was gone.

"Arsenio!" a stern Barber shouted, the banter from the moment before vanishing with the elevator.

"Yes, Your Presidential Highness?"

"What is it you're packing for, fool? We're going to the mattresses! We don't need all this junk."

"A myriad apologies, My President," Arsenio replied, wondering if this would be the last mistake of his life.

He felt the familiar wind burn of a .38 shell passing an inch from his ear. He looked up and saw Barber's sidearm smoking.

"Apology accepted," Barber's response was casual. "Remember the four things I told you can be bartered for anything? Pack up our toilet kits, a couple of changes of underwear and those four things. Got it?"

"Yes, Your Presidential Highness."

Arsenio then went about the task of packing up all the

president's jewels, ammunition, toilet paper and porn.

Newly-promoted Lieutenant General Sanmateo Veecey sat in the Spartan comfort of his wardroom on his battlecraft. He was enjoying the company of his oldest and dearest friend, Benny Goodman.

The King of Swing had, of course, died shortly after Peter Cetera went solo and released *Solitude/Solitaire* and Veecey didn't believe that was coincidence. But Benny Goodman lived on in 'One O'clock Jump', which Veecey and his clarinet had just finished humming out, accompanied by a portable jam-o-mat, a neural-netted synthesizer that impersonates – but doesn't replace – seven-eighths of a jazz octet.

A trip-plate monitor mounted in a corner of the room indicated to him that someone was standing outside his door. So once Veecey blew out the last bar, rested his instrument and pursed his lips to the sound of thunderous synthesized applause, he wasn't surprised by the knock.

"Come!" he called, pressing the pause button on the jam-o-mat.

It was Iman Appdev. She strode in and stood at attention while Veecey undressed her with his eyes, under the pretext of reviewing her military bearing. What a pity, he mused as he rose to his feet, that all that perfection was concealed by a uniform that fit her like a lampshade. Then again, he realized that he found her face captivating as well – despite the metallic ports in and around her mouth, ears and nostrils.

"Report," Veecey chose to say, after discarding, 'Iman, hey, great to see you,' or 'Have you ever braided a man's hair?' or 'I'm rich.'

"We've received new orders, Sir." Crisp as ever, she handed the general a slip of paper.

He looked it over for a moment and made official pronouncement on what she already knew because the duty officer had told her, showed her the document, and sent her on the errand of presenting it to Veecey.

"We're going to Earth."

"Yes, Sir."

"We're rendezvousing with the largest battle group the Eminent Domain has ever fielded."

"Yes, Sir."

"This craft will serve as the flagship for an invasion force of more than three million troops."

Veecey was unable to mask his excitement because, in all honesty, he didn't feel any. Any members of his class at the academy, or any of the members of his extended family who chose military careers, would be staining their jumpsuits at a moment like that. Instead, he just looked blank. The piece of paper could have read, 'Dear High School Senior: Your parents were just killed in a freak accident. Turns out they were broke and uninsured and living on lines of credit for the past ten years and, by the way, your girlfriend is pregnant.'

Time to grow up, he realized. *You can't just hide in the crowd and do a passable job this time. Millions of people are counting on you to not get them killed, Mat, and the fate of two nations rests on your shoulders. You must be single-minded of purpose and deliberate in action. I bet she isn't wearing regulation underwear. Something lacy. And green. Green would look good on her. Any piercing? No, she has too much class. Maybe some ink, though.*

"Dismissed," he said, after censoring the urge to ask, 'Why don't we hang out?' or 'Do you like foot massages?'

She turned on her heel to leave his quarters.

"Lieutenant!" Veecey called out and Appdev halted, turned to face him again and came to attention.

There was an uncomfortable silence as Veecey thought of something to say.

"Appdev, let me ask you a personal question."

"Yes, Sir."

He endeavored to phrase the question with care. Appdev,

he knew, was honest to the point of fanaticism. That was her single unattractive trait. If she were not inclined to accept his proposition, she wouldn't leave it at 'no thank you'. Her Candorian religious precepts would require her to enumerate in thorough detail – ethical, emotional, anatomical – the reasons it wasn't working for her.

"Would you ... how would you like to ... uh...." and the nerve left him. "If you were leader of the band with the best horn section of your era, would you quit to pursue a solo career punctuated by some of the most insipid duets ever recorded?"

"Um ... no?" she replied, unsure. "Sir."

"That's what I thought. Thank you, Appdev."

She left. They would travel light-years together on that battlecraft before he would see her again.

Veecey sat back down, took the jam-o-mat off pause, and launched full-force into 'Stomping at the Savoy.'

☆☆☆

With the invasion set to commence within mere days, M. Griffin Croupier VII was doing his best to get his hands around the enormity of his task. He wasn't getting much help.

He sat in the dim space in the palace basement once known as the War Room, then as the Defense Room, the Situation Room and culminating as the If We Only Knew Then Room. It was shaped like an amphitheater, though much smaller, and he sat in the middle, staring up out of the pit. He was alone, except for the young middle-ranked man in the dashing blue and white uniform of an Eminent Domain Armada officer.

"Whenever you're ready, Commander," Croupier said, placing his glass down on the table beside him and positioning his notepad strategically over his lap.

"Thank you, Sir," the officer began. With a wave of his hand, the lights dimmed even lower.

Without warning, a two-dimensional projection appeared two meters in front of Croupier and about one meter above his eye level. It was a title slide reading, 'Intelligence Briefing to the Foreign Affairs Advisor of the President of the Eminent Domain.' It was subtitled, 'America: What We Know We Don't Know.'

This was followed by a slide of dense agate-typed disclaimers essentially telling the intended audience – Croupier – not to trust any of this information. The footer of the slide read, 'Top Secret and Highly Confidential/Slide 2 of 186.' Croupier stifled a groan.

Two hours later, Slide 145 proved to be the actual intelligence grid. The rows were labeled Military, Government, Culture, History, Geography, Economy, Communications and Logistics.

"At a high level," the commander went on, "here's what we know about America. Despite a history of regional and, at one point, world leadership, it is now engaged in military struggle and alliances of convenience to maintain its territory and identity. Like other Earth cultures, America is no longer a spacefaring nation – although its merchants have been known to book passage on the occasional freighter that passes by – and its technology has devolved to the hydrocarbon or perhaps early nuclear period. This primitiveness has been a barrier to intelligence-gathering, because of the difficulty for those born and raised in the highly-refined Eminent Domain to blend in down there."

"Has it been attempted?" Croupier asked. "I mean, do we have any intelligence assets on the ground there?"

"Not to my knowledge," the officer responded. "Until When All Hell Broke Loose, we never considered it a threat."

"Where would the Terrahists be based?" Croupier asked.

"We believe they are closely affiliated with Barber so, we conjecture, the Terrahists would be likely to infiltrate all the areas still under his control. Our section recommends searching these core American states for WTF."

"What makes you think that?"

"Sorry, Sir?"

"You said, 'we believe' and 'we conjecture.' How do you link Barber and the Terrahists?"

"The president's speeches, Sir."

"Barber's?"

"No, Sir. President Pickfour's. The *real* president."

"And you've confirmed through some kind of primary research that his assertions are correct, right?"

The commander's shining eyes looked less glowing and more glazed.

"That was out of our scope, Sir."

"But you do have other sources of intelligence on America, don't you?"

"Oh yes, Sir. It's all in the appendix."

"Could you walk me through them?"

The commander displayed a color-coded listing of sources.

"OK, let's take out all the movie references," Croupier suggested.

The commander's complex procedure of hand motions erased all the orange text in the grid.

"Now let's remove anything from the editorial page of the *Domestic Diva*," Croupier continued, referring to the broadsheet published by Sajak Pickfour's freshman-year roommate; with that, all the green type disappeared. "And the comics page." The blue text faded out.

"And now let's leave out anything from speeches written or approved by anyone with an office in this building."

In revelation, the grid was blank.

"Lights!" Croupier called and, for the first time, read the nameplate on the commander's uniform: DAYTRADER.

☆☆☆

He couldn't really afford the time off, although he also had to concede he wasn't accomplishing anything at work.

So two hours later, M. Griffin Croupier VII was home in his immaculate kitchen, seasoning up a pot of consommé, listening to the blissful sound from the parlor - his beloved Steve shaking a jigger of martinis. The latest popular high-energy dance anthem was playing at dinner music volume, pouring out of walls which were just floor-to-ceiling speakers in a precise shade of burnt orange.

"As it turns out, he was just another one of Daytrader's nephews," Croupier called from the kitchen. "Never did an intelligence briefing before in his life."

Shake-shake. "What happened to the regular gal?" Shake-shake, was the reply from the parlor.

"Don't ask."

They talked about Steve's day at work for a while - Croupier's job was prestigious but low-paying and Steve's was quite the opposite. He was a judge. To the scant extent he could talk about his work, Steve hated to do so. A short, desultory recap bridged the conversational lull until Steve had the cocktails poured in the everyday-good martini glasses. Had he known how few opportunities he would have to share a quiet drink at home with Griff, maybe he would have broken out the good-good glasses. Steve added one last little flourish to the cocktails, placed them gingerly on a tray and walked them into the closet-sized kitchen.

"... so it was a high-volume, low-margin kind of day," Steve concluded. "But more important, that soup smells almost as good as you do."

"You flatter, kind Sir," Griff replied, a ritual response with origins lost somewhere in their long-ago first dates. Griff was grateful that another ritual of their early days together - Steve's mini-lessons on the history of bartending - had ceased over the past couple of years. After about the hundredth time, it was tiresome to reply 'oh-isn't-that-interesting' to 'cocktails-used-to-contain-depressants-designed-to-impair-your-central-nervous-system.'

"I bet you boiled that water all by yourself," Steve said, offering his tray. "Hard work like that must make a poor waif thirsty."

"Steve!" Griff exclaimed, staring at the martinis' garnishes. "Olives? Real, organic, tree-grown olives? How did you ever find them?"

"How's a man supposed to maintain an air of mystery if he has to answer questions like that?"

"To mystery!" Griff proposed, as they chinked glasses and drank every drop. At that moment, he was sure it was the best martini he'd ever had.

The consommé boiled away into oblivion.

But Croupier's worries didn't. Anyone within the administration who had any knowledge of America – or Earth in general – had been disgraced or worse. The people making the decisions were ideologues who refused to hear inconvenient facts. The troops were going in blind. What kind of climates and terrains would they find in America's various regions? What were the indigenous customs and modes of dress? How did Americans nourish themselves? What was the Barber regime's troop strength? Did they really have the weaponry that Ziglar Tobaccoflack and Reit Daytrader purported, or even the technology to develop it? Did America really support the Terrahists? Did America really murder all those innocent people?

The best martini of Griff Croupier's life was followed by the worst sex.

☆☆☆

"Helloooo?" Emelem Cox-Arquette called into the speaker on his desk as the personal-and-confidential light blinked on.

"Hey there, Uncle!" the tinny filament said, in poor imitation of Watts Barber's booming voice. "Take me off speaker."

"Wattsy-babes, where are you?" Cox-Arquette asked, then took the transceiver off the hook to comply with Barber's request.

"I have to kill anyone I tell," Barber said. "So remind me

before we hang up - I need a few phone numbers."

Cox-Arquette wondered if Barber was kidding.

"Just kidding," the president said, defusing the tension. "Me and Arsenio are somewhere in the Cascades, just going from one safe house to the next. Getting to be a grind. Only so much Oregon I can take."

"So what can I do for my favorite client this fine day?"

"Just calling in for a status report," Barber replied. "Don't know when I'm going to get a chance to call again. How're things going at your end?"

"Peachy - just a big, fuzzy peach," Cox-Arquette said with enthusiasm. "Half the senior staff are already living under assumed names along the Coast. We got an office up and running, or so I'm told. I'm staying here at the Honesty Department building 'til the last minute."

"Way to go. How's Dishy?"

"She's good - all set up in a provisional HQ. Viewed from space though, nobody could tell. The shell game is working, just like you said."

"Great. By this time tomorrow, according to my sources, boots will be hitting the ground. We're going to need the element of surprise."

"You got it, *boychick* ... and how!" Cox-Arquette said.

Barber knew exactly what that façade of enthusiasm meant and mouthed along with Cox-Arquette's next words, verbatim:

"There's just one thing ..."

With a vocal but non-verbal nod from Barber, Cox-Arquette continued.

"... It's great that you know when the invasion's coming, but what are the rest of us supposed to do? Without your contacts, we got no intelligence at all on the Eminent Domain," the Honesty Secretary said. "Dishy keeps asking and I got nothing to give her."

"Cost of doing business," the president replied.

"I never did get that."

"Uncle, you know I trust you more than anyone, right?"

"Of course."

"And I've always given you a seat at the table whenever we needed to bargain with people like Slipfall, right?"

"Right."

"And there weren't no more Americans at that table besides you and me," Barber said, and his tone took a game day turn. "And anyone who had any experience with off-world business when I took over ain't around no more."

"All true," Cox-Arquette said, stifling a tremor in his voice. When Watts Barber took that tone, nobody was safe.

"And I only let you along for the ride because I know you're loyal and I know you're a tough negotiator but, I never let you go anywhere near the spacers unless we were talking about a deal on the table."

"That's right."

"So you think the fact that I'm the only man in America with any four-one-one on anything above breathing level is an accident?"

"No Sirree."

"Yes Siree, no Siree. That's my ace, Uncle," Barber summed up. His tone then turned conspiratorial. "Pickfour's got some huge advantages, but there is a weakness these spacers got that you could tell Dishy about."

"What's that?"

"Take away all the hardware, and they're all just people – regular folk just like us."

☆☆☆

"No intel?" General Camille Dishinstaller asked rhetorically. "How are we supposed to fight without intel?"

"It won't be easy," rasped Lieutenant Colonel Sanjay Sanchez of America's Well Regulated Militia, who, as Dishinstaller's adjutant, considered it his job to answer her rhetorical questions. Accustomed to command – and command of elite forces at that – the gravelly-voiced, careworn officer was still settling into the unfamiliar role of staff aide. It was a career builder, he reminded himself, and temporary.

They sat in the empty shell of her cavernous outer office in Militia Command, just outside the American capital. Dishinstaller's oversized sunglasses hung by a leather cord around her fleshy neck. By this point, ninety percent of the staff had transferred to their insurgency posts, replaced by gelded political prisoners – bound, gagged, injured just enough so they wouldn't die until their heat signatures were no longer needed. Dishinstaller, Sanchez and a few lower-ranking officers were boxing up important files and leaving misinformation behind in the hanging folders. Every map left behind, for instance, would lead not to any top secret installation, or secret WTF lab, but to a small A-frame house in Grand Island, Nebraska, a town where through the entire course of history, nothing ever, ever happened.

That's why she left it as soon as she was old enough to wear the uniform.

"The more we know about them, the more we can exploit their weaknesses," the big-boned general fumed. "And the more we can do that, the fewer of our own troops are going to be lost. So why isn't Barber letting us in on any of their secrets?"

"I guess he doesn't expect the war – or the occupation – to last long," Sanchez replied, his furrowed brow almost lost in the creases and scars that lined his face. "Then, when it blows over, he comes back in a stronger position than ever."

"Yeah, that would be our fearless leader," Dishinstaller said, then sat down under the weight of her overlapping thoughts. "But he's right. How much intel do we really need? Let's just spitball this. It's an occupation force, so everything is going to be controlled from the rear. We already know that the first things they'll want are the plush hotels."

"And so we're abandoning the city. They'll radiate out from here," the colonel continued, grabbing the folding chair next to her. He rolled up his sleeves, revealing the globe-and-anchor symbol of the United States Marine Corps, a branch of service that was subsumed into the Militia the day after Second Lieutenant Sanjay Sanchez got the tattoo.

"Occupation forces are by definition insufficient in number, so it doesn't matter how many they send," the general continued. "At some point, they have to try to win over the population."

"What can they offer?"

"Nothing that's going to last."

"Money?" Sanchez asked. "The whole purpose of an occupation is booty. There's no point in buying out the losers."

"Sure," Dishinstaller speculated. "They're here for the timber, so they'll try to hire anyone they can find who knows how to cut down trees or make pulp."

"If we can't profit from our own resources, we have to make sure our enemies don't either," Sanchez noted.

"Right. Make sure our saboteurs are well away from the front lines when the invasion comes," the general directed, then continued with her original line of thought. "The space monkeys will also have to find some unskilled jobs for the locals."

"Like soldiering?" Sanchez came back, twisting his careworn face into a smile.

But Dishinstaller stared back at him as if he had just issued the most profound pronouncement ever.

"I want half of all front-line units to lay down arms at the first sign of a fight," the general said, rising to pace, and the colonel took out his notepad and paced behind her. "As for those intel specialists whose skills we're not allowed to use, don't you think it's time they found jobs in the hospitality industry?"

☆☆☆

Suffering from both sleep deprivation and sexual frustration, M. Griffin Croupier dragged himself into work extra early the next morning for another critical and important meeting in the If We Only Knew Then Room with President Sajak Pickfour's so-called brain trust: Ambassador Ziglar Tobaccoflack, Admiral Reit Daytrader and Trade Advisor Brosius Slipfall. He marveled that either the word "brain" or "trust" could be used in the same sentence as those names.

It was a budget-and-planning meeting, every bit as boring as that sounded. The next day, they were scheduled to meet with the president and go over it all again.

So Croupier was actually relieved when the meeting was interrupted by an urgent message coming in via videoconf.

"Lieutenant General Veecey!" called out Tobaccoflack as the ponytailed image crystallized. "Congratulations! To what do we owe the pleasure?"

"Ambassador," the general replied with his usual cheer, although everyone in the room could tell he was seething. "Is Admiral Daytrader there with you?"

"Right here, Mat," the admiral said, taking off his green eyeshade. "What can we do for you?"

"Sir, I was just going over the draft rules of engagement you sent me and I'm a little confused."

"I thought they were clear enough." Daytrader was calm, stating a fact, rather than taking umbrage at his orders being questioned.

"I have three million troops, a battle group that could turn the whole planet to ash before breakfast and an enemy that doesn't even have a warning system in orbit, no less an offensive capability."

"You need more troops?" Daytrader asked. "Next year's budget planning starts in just a couple ..."

"Sir, I could do the job with just the security detail you gave me, if these rules of engagement were less, um, stringent."

"There are reasons for the stringency," the admiral said. "They're not strictly military. Griff? Mat, this is Griff Croupier. He's heading this up from a policy perspective."

Croupier had been dreading this conversation, although he'd known for some time it was coming. He was now looking at the soldier who was charged with carrying out the plan which was finalized in that room. Croupier had seen pictures of Sanmateo Veecey before - clean-cut, clear-eyed, confident. They were, of course, taken earlier in his career and didn't look anything like the image on the screen at that moment. Croupier was taken by surprise, having never seen a general with hair that long.

"We're not going to burn Earth to a cinder, General," Croupier said. "You were able to resolve the Fifty-five Cancri crisis with a more restrained approach, and we're counting on you to do the same here."

"Fine, Mister Croupier, I understand not frying the planet from space. But no post-nuclear ground-based weapons?"

"You'll still have an overwhelming technological advantage," interjected Slipfall. "They're still using firearms and car bombs. Last thing we need is another galaxy-wide have/have-not guilt-fest. Very bad for business."

"Sorry. Who was that?"

"Brosius Slipfall. Trade," he said by way of introduction and was just about to launch into an unrequested defense of eschewing ecologically devastating tactics on a planet so rich in natural resources. "You see …"

"OK, I suppose that makes sense, Mister Slipfall," the general said, cutting him off. "But if that's the case, I'll need more troops."

"Mat, you've got more troops than have ever been assigned to a single officer. Do you know how many three million is?"

"Sir, do you know how big America is?" Veecey asked back, then continued after a pregnant pause. "That troop level will be fine for an invasion, Sir, but what about the occupation? How long are we going to be occupying America?"

"First, we're liberating, not occupying," Ambassador

Tobaccoflack corrected. "Second, we're not going to be staying long. We take out Watts Barber, install a responsible, democratically-elected puppet government and fly away home."

"What if they don't want to be liberated?" Veecey wondered aloud. "What if they prefer a homegrown dictator to a legitimate government dozens of light years away? We could get bogged down in a guerrilla war that ends only when we finally give up."

"General, General," Tobaccoflack said, with the subtext of just-go-tune-your-clarinet. "We've table-topped this for months. We've planned for every contingency, considered every possible outcome and the scenario you present is just so far outside the realms of likelihood, that it was dismissed very early in the process. Why ... you're the first person at this level of responsibility to ever raise the point."

"Fact is, Mat, I'd love to give you more troops, but we just don't have them," Daytrader said, nudging the ambassador out of the frame. "We have other priorities: the mutual defense pact with the Associated Market, our ongoing rivalry with the Kleptocosm, the possibility of unconventional war coming from any of hundreds of other planets. Sorry, but you'll just have to make do."

"Yes, Sir," Veecey said with a sigh.

ASTONISHMENT

General Veecey stood captivated, as he watched the display. In zero-gee, held in place by magnets rather than a planet's pull, he had the odd feeling he *was* the airborne drone, observing the American wilds from treetop height. Really though, he was just screening the visual data in a room crowded with technicians and technocrats, all bustling about or clamoring for his attention.

He wasn't the drone, of course, nor was he even directing its flight. The bird - that's what they called it, and that's what it looked like - flew itself, although there was a technical sergeant seated at the control panel in front of Veecey and Iman Appdev, who were hovering nearby. Iman, now Captain Appdev, found her new role as Veecey's adjutant challenging, and was happy to not have to wear the sensory implants anymore. Veecey noticed how her complexion, smooth and supple to begin with, glowed creamy radiance now that it was exposed to air, starlight and gene therapy. Staring at her face, he could forget for a moment what a risk he was taking putting a Candorian - whose compulsive truth-telling made her a valuable intelligence officer - in the kind of staff position that called for discretion and tact.

They all watched the screen as the forests gave way to hills. Then the hills gave way to mountains; mountains sloped down to flatlands. All the while, wilderness gave way to settlements, which yielded to roads, which led to towns and, eventually, on the horizon, a glimmer of a city. This city, the American capital, reflected a polished glaze even at that distance and altitude. As the drone closed in, the general and his subordinates could make out the distinctive skyline, then the outlines of the individual buildings. Veecey knew the names of half of them even before he'd read his briefing materials for this mission. It filled him with wonderment to know that he would soon see these buildings up close, that he would soon enter them. Still, even in lunar orbit, he was overwhelmed by the legend of the city as a whole – the ancient seat of American power, the crowning glory of American pride.

Las Vegas.

"There's the White House," Appdev marveled aloud, as Veecey remembered from school days that it was once called the Bellagio.

"And there's Congress, Sir," the technical sergeant said, as Veecey remembered it used to be called the Chicken Ranch.

The streets of Las Vegas were abandoned. The town was boarded up – all except for the notorious always-open casinos, which dimmed their lights but kept their doors open. An assortment of ethnic restaurants let diners in through unblocked kitchen doors. Quite a number of liquor stores and beer distributors had their back-alley lights on too. One house at the edge of town had its windows wide open, colored lights pouring out, the house's voluptuous female occupants wearing helmets and fragmentation vests and little else.

Still, it was next to impossible to buy groceries.

The tiny bird flew undetected around the city at low altitude three times then headed back through the upper atmosphere, reached escape velocity, kept accelerating and eight hours later, returned to the general's command-and-control vessel, parked in synchronous orbit over the dark side of the moon.

If it could hear as well as see, the drone would have perceived Veecey's address to the troops he was about to send into harm's way or, as he liked to think of it, lead into battle.

"People," he began, as his ponytail whipped wildly in the microgravity, "today we embark on a crusade. We will draw upon all the vast resources at our disposal. We will attack with all the righteous fury in our souls. And we will deploy the ultimate weapon in our arsenal ...

Astonishment."

He paused to let the word sink into a million pairs of ears on a thousand ships. He brushed an attack of conscience from his soul and a long strand of hair from his eyes. *Sell it, Mat, sell it,* he told himself. *If you believe it, they'll believe it.*

"The enemy shall look to the sky and be astounded, amazed and utterly dumbfounded. We will astonish the enemy in his home. We will astonish him in the street. We will astonish him in the market. Night after night and day after day, we will rain stupefaction down from the heavens. There is only so much spectacle a man can take before he capitulates to superior powers of incredulity. The enemy, driven underground by the sheer force of bewilderment, will emerge from the depths wearing a mask of bafflement, and slink, sluggish, toward his conquerors under the white flag of befuddlement.

"So before we risk even a single member of this vanguard on a ground assault, we have a surprise in store for the enemy."

An expanse of darkness wrapped the American capital in a moonless night, the Strip's usual brilliance eerily extinguished.

The lights from the sky came first. Primary colors streaked across the blackened firmament, forming bars and wheels that swooped with impossible speed toward the ground then back up to the heavens. They formed more complex shapes - first scalene triangles and tetrahedrons, then rhombahedrons, truncated octahedrons and icosidodecahedrons. Primary colors blurred into more subtle hues - persimmon, hot plum, melaleuca. These forms spun wildly, danced, merged and exploded in bursts of laser-simulated pyrotechnics.

Up in his flagship, General Veecey watched with pride and guarded optimism. This might work after all.

"Captain, initiate Phase Bingo," he ordered Appdev, grateful to have something fascinating upon which to rest his gaze, besides the forbidden form of the woman he desired but could never possess. *My own little touch.*

"Phase Bingo, yessir," Appdev replied. "Sergeant, initiate Phase Bingo."

"Phase Bingo is go, Ma'am," the sergeant reported back as he pressed a single button.

Sound built. Drumbeats swelled from distant thumps to ear-splitting interpretations of approaching cannon. Layers of upright bass, electric guitar and synthesizer joined the light show. A multipart vocal chorus joined in, singing "aaaaahs" and "mmmmmms" and at length adding lyrics. The words conveyed masterful, meaningful poetry, even though they were masked by the percussion, the harmonies and obscure accents.

☆☆☆

General Veecey, who might have been the only one on the ground or in space who knew the lyrics, had turned off the electromagnets in his boots and was floating about the wardroom. He stared out into space, literally.

"General?" Appdev probed, approaching him after what she considered an appropriate interval for a commander to be reflecting on larger issues.

"Yes, Captain?"

"That music," she inquired. "Classical?"

"Yes."

"It's amazing. What is it?"

"Pink Floyd," he responded wistfully. "I don't know why. It just seemed to fit."

"Yes, Sir."

"Anything else?"

"No, Sir."

"Then let's all get back to business," the general replied. "Let's astonish them back to the Stone Age."

☆☆☆

It didn't work. Astonishing the population of Las Vegas turned out to be harder than drowning a fish.

No white flag came up. America's Well Regulated Militia took up defensive positions. They would leave it to later generations to judge whether they erred in using universally accepted neutral sanctuaries as cover, as they set up strongholds in every chapel, casino and bordello.

The ground war began. The Americans had superior numbers and the home court advantage, but the

Domestic troops brought more than compensatory firepower.

Jumping into downtown Las Vegas, still, was out of the question. Veecey's ground troops landed at sites out of range of the capital's antispacecraft barrages, touching down deep in the Mojave Desert.

They met with stronger resistance than anticipated. There was little sincerity behind small-town smiles.

People could hide their true selves; the desert could not. More than a hundred Domestic soldiers learned through rapid attrition why the area between the landing zone and Las Vegas was called Death Valley.

One of those soldiers was Private Coder, 89164B26M. Underneath the tinted visor of his helmet, he bore a remarkable resemblance to the MetLifeWorlder who was famously misled about the chance of rain When All Hell Broke Loose. That was because they were clones, comprised of the same genetic material and mass-produced as menial laborers and cannon fodder.

Considered expendable, they were often used by Domestic military tacticians to draw fire from rights-holding Domestic soldiers. As part of their battle dress uniform, they were all issued bright red tunics.

With his entire spaceborne division, Coder jumped out of the transport at one thousand meters, his descent slowed by jetpack. As soon as he was clear of the transport, he removed his helmet.

Smarter than many, Coder extended his life somewhat by not wearing his helmet. He reasoned that, if attacking from above, there was little chance he would be shot in the head. In the vain hope that he might pass his genetic gifts on in a more traditional way than he himself received them, he held the helmet with his knees, keeping it between Earth and his reproductive system.

At three hundred meters, he saw two members of his platoon shredded by primitive ballistic weaponry that bounced painfully, but without causing harm, off his redeployed headgear.

The fight began when the spaceborne division made landfall at 0448, local time. The Domestic troops were pounded by artillery but regrouped with valiant immediacy under fire and brought their general-issue DT100,000 Raysprayers to bear. By 0458, the tide had turned in the Domestic troops' favor and it was at 0500 on the dot that the Americans surrendered.

It all seemed too rehearsed, too well-timed for Coder. It was.

How the Americans came to be along that route at that hour would one day be cause for scandal. That they surrendered right at the top of the hour lent the appearance that they intended to lose this fight all along.

Coder's misgivings, though, went unrecorded. Not five seconds after tens of thousands of Americans said "I surrender" in unison and threw down their arms, one last projectile – an old-time rifle shell – pierced Coder's neck.

As he lay there, blood leaking like dye from his red shirt, his consciousness and life seeping away, he heard one American call out to a compatriot:

"What did you do that for? Don't you read your e-mail?"

☆☆☆

Veecey's battle plan called for a swift advance into the capital, but it was not to be. Unexpectedly fierce resistance, followed by the logistical nightmare of processing a sudden influx of surrendering combatants, the midsummer desert heat, the faulty equipment supplied by Admiral Daytrader's cousin without competitive bid, all contributed to slow, slogging progress.

Judging by the broadcasts sent from the American Department of Honesty, one wouldn't even know there was a war on.

"The attack hasn't begun yet," Honesty Secretary Emelem Cox-Arquette told the viewing audience as the astonishment show blazed overhead for a third straight night.

"We've captured a small band of reconnaissance troops and are interrogating them now," Cox-Arquette said, as firefights raged in the Mojave.

"The Domestic president is already suing for peace. His band of bloodthirsty renegades will never enter the capital," Cox-Arquette said, as the thunder of artillery echoed off Hoover Dam.

"I'll tell him you stopped by but the secretary is out this morning, playing golf at Desert Pines," Cox-Arquette's receptionist told General Veecey as he strode into the Honesty building, surrounded by a platoon-strength security detail. "He shot a sixty-eight last week."

The general just stood there, glum. He had more to worry about than ferreting out one annoying propagandist, who was far from the only member of the American government to escape capture during the assault on Las Vegas. Watts Barber himself was at the top of that list. The general knew this was one of a litany of inconvenient truths he couldn't take to President Pickfour.

And Sanmateo Veecey was concerned less with Barber's whereabouts than with those of his own opposite number, General Camille Dishinstaller. Far from being Barber's lackey, a word which described most of the civilian officials, Dishinstaller was a veteran war fighter and a danger in her own right. Most of her senior staff and field commanders were also still at large, the core of America's professional Well Regulated Militia. And many of them had served with her since before Watts Barber was president, when he was merely a King.

Oh well, he consoled himself, wiping the sweat from under his ponytail, *at least it introduced another generation to Pink Floyd.*

So the youthful, stubble-chinned American man who showed up days later at the Bellagio looking for work at the occupation's hastily-converted headquarters was humming 'Wish You Were Here.'

He waited in line for three hours to see a Domestic sergeant seated at a tiny desk in the middle of a big ballroom. The sergeant's harried demeanor and bloodshot eyes spoke to the three-hour line that still remained.

The American gave a name, any name.

"Can you drive a hover car?" the sergeant asked.

"No, Sir," the American said, with a dejected expression.

"Any police or security experience?"

"None, Sir."

"Any skills at all?" the sergeant asked, annoyance driving the boredom out of his voice.

"I worked in restaurants," the American said, his clear blue eyes brightening. "I can wait tables. Or I can work in the kitchen. Do you need a short order cook?"

The sergeant rolled his eyes.

☆☆☆

Once his job was done and the civilian leadership was ensconced in certain friendly regions of southern California, Emelem Cox-Arquette made some calls, moved some accounts around, cashed in a couple of favors, whispered in receptive ears, did lunch at the right places and the results were predictable. Every one of Watts Barber's flunkies at a high enough level to be a threat to Cox-Arquette was arrested, murdered, or endlessly photographed in unflattering light.

There was soon nobody left to run the internally-exiled government except him, Emelem Cox-Arquette, luxuriating in his ancestral estate in the ancient holy city of Hollywood.

MISSION ACCOMPLISHED

What have we got left?" a blue-jeaned and sweat-shirted General Camille Dishinstaller asked a bedraggled Lieutenant Colonel Sanjay Sanchez, standing before her desk at insurgency headquarters. Behind her, on the wall of the one-time Bubbling Wells Elementary School in Palm Springs, were Old Glory and the banner of the Well Regulated Militia. The battle-scarred colonel was still in his Militia uniform, whether too busy or too sentimental to change into the civilian garb of a guerilla war, the general couldn't tell. But it had been a month since American forces had been chased out of Las Vegas and this was neither the time, nor place, for nostalgia.

"Just about everything, Ma'am. They hold the Vegas Strip. Also, they have garrisons in every major city," he said. "But surrendering enough soldiers and materiel to convince the enemy they were winning was a master stroke. We still got about three-quarters of a functional army."

"Thank you, Colonel. Oh, and remember to change into civvies today," she said, wiping a smudge from her sunglasses. "It'll be a long time before we get to wear battledress again. Dismissed."

He snapped to attention, saluted, turned and marched out, striding over an up-ended sand table. Dishinstaller looked down her clipboard.

"Next! Major ... Celltower?"

A clear-eyed but stubble-chinned young man stepped past the frosted-glass door and snapped to. He wore casual civilian clothes with a waiter's apron tucked under his arm, but carried himself with the bearing of a career officer of the Well Regulated Militia.

"Major G.Q. Celltower reporting as ordered, Ma'am," said the man, wide-eyed, his voice conveying boundless enthusiasm.

Dishinstaller knew that look. Thirty years and thirty pounds ago, she still couldn't have seduced a gorgeous man like that. And yet men like Celltower lined up to salute her. Her life of service to her country may have left her lonely but she was one of the few women in American history who knew – for a fact – that legions of men respected her for her professional competence and leadership. She found that respect very gratifying and, when she was being honest with herself, considered it even more gratifying than anything else they could give her.

"At ease. You're our inside man at Eminent Domain Occupation Command, right?"

"Yes, Ma'am, but they don't call it that," Celltower reported. "In deference to the hundred forty-three soldiers sent by Grand Organ powers allied with the Eminent Domain, they refer to their HQ as 'Friends Helping Friends Civilize America. Suggestions Welcomed,' Ma'am."

"Troop strength?"

"Between HQ and local garrisons, they're fielding some- where above two million combat troops and the usual complement of support personnel, Ma'am, plus the crews up in orbit."

"So we're not outmanned. Are we outgunned?"

"Request permission to speak frankly, Ma'am."

At the general's nod, Celltower dropped the military

bearing.

"If they really want to drop the hammer they can do it from space," he said, arching his thick eyebrows and cocking his head. "They haven't. If they wanted to win a ground war with overpowering force, they could have brought in ten times the troop strength they have deployed today. We figure these half-measures are due to political concerns."

"The Grand Organ?"

"No, Ma'am. As far as I can tell, Pickfour couldn't care less about the other worlds. But he's got an election coming up and he can't end the war until it's over."

"I'm not following."

"He hasn't committed the troops and tech to do the job right because of a Domestic superstition: They won't replace their president during a war."

"So the longer the war ..."

"... the longer his term. Yes Ma'am."

"That's logic worthy of our own leader. By the way, any word on whether they caught President Barber yet?"

"No word, Ma'am."

"Then you can bet," she said, rising to turn and face the faded Stars and Stripes, "they have no more idea where he is than we do."

☆☆☆

The galacticam news channel was broadcasting live from the erstwhile White House, now rechristened Friends Helping Friends Headquarters but still popularly called the Bellagio.

Veecey was trying to carry on with his early morning briefing in the conference room adjacent to his office, but the news crew was even more obtrusive than his security detail. He didn't want them there, but he was overruled. Ziglar Tobaccoflack, the head of the Domestic Diplomatic Corps, had orchestrated their total access. Tobaccoflack himself, had a weakness for the media - an outgrowth, perhaps, of his weakness for acclaim. A one-time child star, he became a daytime drama star, a nighttime comedy star, a live-cast theater star, not to mention an infomercial star. It wasn't until after he was a news star that Tobaccoflack set his sights on being a political star. Now he was a member of Sajak Pickfour's Steering Committee and clearly on the ascent. And he was adamant about galacticam access. ('Don't worry, it won't last too long,' he had told Veecey via comnet a couple of days before. 'It's just through-sweeps week.')

Veecey couldn't send the crew home, but he could impose upon the producer to limit the number of people in the room. No problem, the producer had told Veecey, the only crew members who needed to be in the room were herself, the news star of course, the cam op, sound tech, light tech, technical director, makeup artist and each of their assistants. The interns could wait in the hovertruck.

It still seemed crowded to Veecey.

"How many did we lose?" he asked one of a half dozen staff officers seated around the table, with the dawn refracting through the gleaming glass of water set at each place. All chairs were pulled in as close to the table as the officers could manage, to make room for the news crew.

"Casualties were light, Sir," the aide replied. "Two-hundred-twelve killed."

Veecey nodded, but he displayed no expression beyond his usual cocked head and wandering glance. He often looked distracted and nobody at the table could reckon what was behind the mask. Cold calculation? Deep sadness? Wistful nostalgia for less burdensome times? Did he even understand what he'd just been told?

It happened to be deep sadness. Two-hundred-twelve was still too many. He didn't go into the military to send notes home to the families. He went into the military, initially, to play in the band.

"Acceptable," he said, squeezing as much conviction as he could muster into that word. "We planned for ten times that."

An antigrav microphone hovering over the table inexplicably rocketed straight up into the chandelier. A moment later, it was raining crystal.

"Sorry," the sound tech said, unconvincing to anyone who heard.

"We've taken as many hits as we thought we would but battlefield medicine has come a long way," another aide said. "We've been able to patch them up pretty good."

Veecey nodded in acknowledgment then turned to Appdev.

"Captain, any truth to the rumors of an insurgency forming?"

"Nothing we can confirm yet, General, but very likely yes," Appdev reported in a casual, affable voice. Veecey felt the warmth flow from his auditory canals through his brain, down his spine and out through every nerve. "There's been some chatter to that effect. It's coming primarily from southern California and the northern Plains. We expected to have some mopping up to do once major combat was over."

She stopped talking, meaning she had summarized everything she knew on the subject. Veecey, in turn, said nothing, just stared and tried to mask his longing for the doe-eyed beauty in fatigues.

It took him a minute, but he was able to focus on his responsibilities again. He twisted a lock of his ponytail in a pre-arranged signal to an aide who was less scrupulously honest than Appdev.

It was time to get rid of the galacticam crew.

"Sir?" the aide interjected.

The cam spun around to zoom in on the aide, cracking an Obama Dynasty vase in the process, followed by another hollow 'sorry' as water and fresh-cut flowers spilled on the carpet.

"Uh, you asked me to let you know when it's oh-seven-hundred."

Spotlight. Lamp. "Sorry."

"Thank you, Lieutenant," Veecey said, ignoring the latest crash. "I wanted to keep track of when the blackjack tables open."

Suddenly, the galacticam crew had somewhere else to be.

"Do we have enough footage, you think?" the news star asked his producer.

"Oh, sure," she replied. "We just wanted some stock images. Wow, is it that late? Where does the time go? C'mon, people, let's let these brave warriors do their, uh, meeting."

The entire crew hastened out of the door at once with their equipment and promptly wrecked a slot machine beyond repair, for which they apologized. The casino's centuries-old scent of cigarette smoke and whores' perfume rushed in until someone shut the door.

Once the news team was well down the hall on its way to the casino, the aide who reported the casualty figures dropped her pretense of confidence and capability, as her shoulders hunched up and her face fell to her hands.

"We are so screwed!" she said, almost sobbing.

"It was like a coffee grinder out there," added the officer who spoke about battlefield medicine. He then stammered in disbelief, "Did you hear ... what happened to battalion HQ in Sioux City? They were overrun! General, the bandits ... beheaded ... some of our troops!"

"Barbaric," Veecey said, knowing that didn't begin to cover it. "Appdev, what about Dishinstaller? Do we know where she is?"

"We think she's heading up the California contingent," Appdev said crisply.

"I figured," Veecey replied. "From what little we know about her, she's a professional, not a sadist."

Appdev had, weeks earlier, briefed Veecey on Dishinstaller's family background – that she was raised in a working-class family in Grand Island, Nebraska. Appdev was also aware that Veecey knew about her stellar performance at the military academy, her distinguished service record and her reputation as an unpredictable tactician.

"She almost certainly had nothing to do with beheading anyone, Sir," Appdev responded. "At the Battle of Walt Disney World, she caught one of her own soldiers decapitating a Floridian separatist and had him disciplined in the most ..."

"Walt Disney World?" Veecey inquired. "Don't you mean 'WaltDisneyWorldWorld'?"

"No, Sir," Appdev said. "There's a place in Florida with a similar name."

"I hope it's as nice," Veecey said, suddenly wistful for a planet he spent so many happy days on as a boy. "If we could take these Americans off this horrific planet and show them what would be available to them if they allied themselves with the Eminent Domain, all resistance would peter out in short order. I wonder if Dishinstaller ever visited WaltDisneyWorldWorld."

"No, Sir, I'm sure she hasn't," Appdev replied.

"Explain."

"According to all records, she's never been off Earth in her life."

"Really? Never? Then she's got no idea how we live or what our customs are," Veecey conjectured. "She's going to have to rely heavily on intelligence gathering. Get the word out to the troops to watch themselves around any locals."

All the aides nodded in agreement.

"How about the civilian government?" Veecey asked, on to the next topic. "Do we know where Barber is? Cox-Arquette? Any of the other top suits?"

"No clue, Sir," one of the aides chimed in after a long silence.

"Get on it," the general ordered. "In the best case, they've disbanded. In the worst case, they're behind the fanatics in the northern Plains. I want to know either way."

Orders were cut and distributed to all troops under General Sanmateo Veecey's command: Don't share any information about the Domestic way of life with any indigenous Americans.

It came within hours of orders related to proper display of the campaign ribbon, regulation spacing of dress uniform belt buckle holes and the most orderly and efficient manner of tying boot laces.

And that new room service waiter at the Bellagio was, in many estimations, just *so cute.*

"Enough of all this stuff about strategy and position and troop movements and stuff," President Pickfour told his Steering Committee. "We need a nickname."

"A nickname?" Ambassador Tobaccoflack inquired as he managed, in deference to his president, to look away from the council room's ornate, mirrored walls. "For whom?"

"The Americans," the president replied. "It's a tradition."

Nobody said anything. They just exchanged furtive glances.

"Throughout Earth history, nations have invented nicknames ..." the president said, then glanced down at the Word-A-Day calendar on his desk, "... *derogatory* nicknames to dehumanize the enemy. For example, the Chinese were called Charlie. The Germans were called Jerry. The French were called ... um, Lucky, what was it the French were called?"

"Pussy."

"Oh yes, right," the president continued. "Pussy. It was on the tip of my tongue. Now what are we going to call the Americans?"

"Um, McBudweiser?" inquired one tentative aide.

"Stadium blimps?" someone volunteered over the clinking of ice water being poured into a tumbler.

"Wal-Martians?" came a voice from the back.

Then came the deluge.

After about twenty minutes, well maybe thirty - certainly under an hour - the topic wore itself out. Pickfour then went with the idea he'd had before even calling the meeting. And it was the perfect nickname: distinctly American and a withering insult.

"So do y'all like it?" the president asked, rhetorically of course, before singling out Croupier for the official consensus. "What do you think, Lucky?"

"Very good, Sir," Croupier said, with the great confidence of one who believes the powerful truly respects his opinion. "And while we're on the subject of horrible nicknames ..."

Croupier spoke his mind. President Pickfour never called him 'Lucky' again. Instead, Croupier found himself on the next transport to Earth demoted once more, this time to Viceroy of America.

He would have just hours to bid Steve farewell, settle into his new circumstances and be briefed by General Veecey on the extent of the small insurgency that would, every so often, shatter the peace.

Mere days after Croupier's arrival, the president and some of his entourage paid a surprise visit to Las Vegas to tell the troops in person of the bold new epithet.

☆☆☆

Ambassador Ziglar Tobaccoflack accompanied his president to America. He didn't want to - space travel left him with bags under his eyes - but the president was insistent.

"Ziggy, I need you on this one," President Sajak Pickfour told him just before the trip was announced to the press. "I need to convey a sense of righteousness, resoluteness, strengthfulness. And you are my administration's greatest authority on conveying."

Tobaccoflack had enough money, power and adulation to never need any more. And it was true enough that he didn't crave money or power. He was, though, a sucker for compliments.

Sajak Pickfour, the most powerful man in the galaxy, followed up greatest-authority-on-conveying with a proper nod to Tobaccoflack's new low-gee wingtips. The celebrity diplomat bought them because they offered the illusion of another two centimeters of height when, in fact, he was just hovering that much off the carpet. But the president saw past that and remarked on how the cordovan complemented the color of his shirt and how the lines were retro without being kitschy.

An hour later, Tobaccoflack was packing his suitcase, humming a happy tune.

☆☆☆

Coder, 25Q10N60S, was on patrol in Kansas City until, in an instant, he wasn't anymore. The tracking equipment used by Domestic troops in the rear was notoriously buggy and there always seemed to be some atmospheric disturbance or another interfering with the positioning equipment aboard the ships in orbit.

Coder was found days later in Omaha. Mostly.

Some of him was in Dubuque. Some of him was in Peoria.

His red shirt was run up a flagpole outside Indianapolis.

☆☆☆

"This is a great day, Mister President," Tobaccoflack said, as he helped President Sajak Pickfour with his hair and makeup. The lighting in the green room in the Friends Helping Friends armory was dim except for the magnifying mirror that reflected the president's face, pore by pore. "Truly momentous. You should be proud."

"Honest, Ziggy, I'm humbled. Humbled, in the way that only a man who's taken the resources of five hundred worlds to beat the defenses of a nation that occupied a quarter of a continent, can understand."

"Whatever you say, Sir. Here, have a sip of water."

"Thanks, Zigs,' he said, when he was done teething on the straw. "I'm just so privileged to bask in the presence of these brave and courageous folk who are defending us so nobly and honorably."

A beefy member of the presidential guard stuck his head in the green room and announced, "It's almost time, Mister President."

"Thank you, Nealon," Pickfour said as he arose, took the protective cheesecloth out of his collar and stood there, admiring how dashing he looked in the flight suit it was his prerogative to wear. He turned his back to Tobaccoflack and asked, "Ziggy, could you give me a zip up?"

"Sir, um, the zipper goes in front."

It was a short stride down a poured-concrete corridor to the armory's central hall. Pickfour, flanked by aides and members of his security detail, arrived to hear Croupier concluding his speech.

"... so I look forward to working in close proximity with General Veecey to bring us all home someday soon, intact and with honor. But I'm not the reason you've assembled here today. Without further ado, I give you the architect of the Friends Helping Friends initiative, the liberator of America, our bold and decisive leader, the Most Honorable President of the Eminent Domain, Sajak Pickfour!"

The applause and cheers were enthusiastic, riotous. They went on for long minutes. At last, the three thousand troops assembled in the hall settled into their chairs, yet the cheers went on unabated. Then a red-faced audio technician flicked a switch and they stopped.

After a few prefatory remarks heaping compliment after compliment on the assembled troops, extending fulsome praise to Croupier and to Veecey, who was also in attendance, the president got to the point of his address.

"Elvis!"

Three thousand troops heard that word in person, as three million more viewed the address via comnet from forward posts.

"Elvis!" Pickfour repeated for effect. Croupier and Veecey were seated, mute, behind him on the dais, Tobaccoflack smiling triumphantly from the wings. "You want to know who resisted our attempts to establish a civilized government here? It was Elvis! Who are the cowards behind this vicious insurgency that keeps us here and prevents us from going home to our loved ones? That's Elvis too! Who are we going to pursue and disable and torture and destroy until he's free?"

"Elvis!" Three thousand voices responded in unison. Anyone in the room could feel the electricity – the eagerness in the troops to return to their duty and bring down the bad guy.

He's right, Croupier thought. *It's working. Pickfour may be as dumb as a tree trunk, but he guessed right yet again!*

Confetti fell from the high ceiling, while rolls of multi-hued streamers unraveled as they sailed through the air. A laser show that Veecey himself had a hand in designing, lit up as a backdrop behind the president spelling out, in letters taller than the tallest men in the room, 'WE WIN.' The letters morphed into a new slogan: 'EVERYBODY LOVES US,' then 'YOU WANT SOME MORE, ELVIS?' followed by 'BITE MY ASS, AMERICA.'

Croupier noticed a man carrying a tray of water pitchers, a very good-looking man with a sexy growth of stubble, moving toward the Serene Avenue exit at that point. Croupier didn't pay him much regard. The young man wasn't with the Domestic forces. He was probably just a local civilian contractor. Maybe he took some offense at all this 'Elvis' business. Maybe he was just going off duty. Croupier dismissed him as just another American pissboy. *Nice tush, though.*

It wasn't the last Croupier would see of G.Q. Celltower.

The president didn't stay long.

Less than an hour later, he was on a shuttle that would take him to a transport that would whisk him back to the Eminent Domain, where Admiral Reit Daytrader was holding down the fort. Now that major combat was officially over, Daytrader was seeing to it that combat pay was likewise canceled.

On the president's transport, Tobaccoflack convinced him to meet, as soon as they arrived, with a delegation from the American expatriate community. Tens of thousands of Domestic residents hailed from pre-Barber America and, indeed, many billions traced their ancestry back to that benighted land.

And some had taken offense. Not at the military operation, because most Americans living in exile were vehement in their opposition to the Barber regime. But they didn't care for the Elvis caricature.

Immediately after the president's speech, the anti-American image of a fat, middle-aged man in a sequined jumpsuit, mutton-chop sideburns, a pompadour and oversized sunglasses popped up in the media, from graffiti to political cartoons. The obscure regional dialect of the historical Elvis was used by the cybernetic media to denote any American.

The expatriates wanted to set the record straight. They informed the president that the American public didn't dress like that, wear their hair like that or speak like that. They certainly didn't swivel their hips or karate-chop the air like that.

These modes and mannerisms were not representative of the average American, they explained, and were reserved strictly for the clergy.

Some American-Domestic activists made that point quite clear a few days later. That's when they marched on the presidential palace – or, at least, to the outermost guardhouse, along the service road, through the minefield, on the way to the back door of the servants' quarters, adjacent to the grounds of the presidential palace, which is as close as they got.

After presenting their point to an assistant to the acting adjunct deputy under-minister who met them cordially, listened politely, promised sincerely to do everything she could for them and declined apologetically to validate their parking, the marchers adjourned to a series of open-air cafés along a distinguished, embassy-studded avenue.

It was near the end of the day and the marchers began to mingle with the usual after-work crowd. As modest as their success was, they did more in two hours to sway Domestic public opinion over drinks and sketches on paper napkins than they did all day screaming for the galacticam drones.

One American-born permanent resident in particular, was having great success with one Domestic citizen, in particular.

"... so you see, this entire war was unprovoked," said the American man with broad shoulders carried with pride on an upright spine, his soulful, weary eyes staring deep into the dazzled gaze of the man across the table. "As much as we hate Watts Barber - and many of us would rise up against him if we felt we had the support - we can't tolerate foreign troops on our soil and we don't want to host another war."

He paused for a sip from his drink.

"Man, I'm dying for some real, American, food," he told the spellbound local. "Ever have a hamburger?"

"Who? Me? No!" the Domestic man replied and blushed a little.

"Hey, you're kind of cute," the American said, intuiting that they were aligned on the same side of the Lane-Broderick scale. "What's your name?"

The Domestic man flushed from cheek to cheek as he shyly replied, "Steve."

ELVIS LIVES

The Eminent Domain-led Friends Helping Friends coalition didn't just think they were winning the war. They thought they'd won it.

That notion came to an abrupt end one warm, sunny day in the brown skies over the American holy city of Hollywood. An airplane sputtered along at low altitude over the hills and cast a shadow over the Friends Helping Friends garrison, once known as the Playboy Mansion. Friends Helping Friends functionaries heard the rattling sound and roused themselves from their desks, their grottoes, their rotating beds, and looked up. In those days of gravity-resistant hovercraft, kerosene-powered planes were anachronistic. This creaky passenger jet must be some kind of publicity stunt, the occupiers thought, maybe an Old Hollywood type trying to drum up business for some sordid enterprise that relied on the Eminent Domain's well-paid troops and better-paid contractors.

"A jet airplane being used as a weapon?" asked one startled soldier lucky enough, up to that point, to be billeted there. "Who ever heard of *that?*"

The erstwhile lucky private standing next to him, Coder, 38111T61S, had. Coder's favorite galacticam shows were all on such outlets as The Violence Channel, Deathtime, Sausagegrinder and Mayhem, so he was better informed. But all that knowledge left him a scant moment later as his red shirt was repeatedly drilled by shrapnel.

☆☆☆

"What the hell happened?" General Sanmateo Veecey demanded, hurdling over his molded-plastic desk as soon as the video feed reached his HQ at the former Bellagio.

"Still assessing damage, Sir," replied Captain Iman Appdev, ever close but ever unattainable, supervising a row of prosthetically-enhanced intel specialists in Veecey's outer office.

"I want a briefing in five minutes," he said, then stormed back into his private room, slamming the door behind him in a rare display of temper.

He had calmed down sufficiently when Appdev peered in exactly three hundred seconds later. She could read the general's face though, and knew that his rage was barely subdued. A nod from him was all the command she needed to begin the briefing.

"An antique aircraft called a 'seven-thirty-seven' took off from a field or highway somewhere between Hollywood, Palm Springs and San Diego."

"Haven't we known since we got here that there might be insurgents hiding in that area?"

"Yes, Sir. Our intel people call it the 'Sunny Triangle.' A seven-thirty-seven can carry between as many as ..."

"Is it a military aircraft?"

"This was some kind of workhorse, short-haul passenger jet dating back to the DOS Age," she said. "Somewhere around one hundred insurgents crammed aboard and jumped out – without parachutes – at an altitude of approximately two hundred meters, through what we speculate were their boarding doors. In an improvised attack pattern, they set off fifty kilograms each of a high explosive, yet to be determined, using a trigger mechanism, yet to be determined. The explosives propelled what we believe to be nails, bolts or industrial staples. The resultant trauma to vital organs caused massive loss of blood and function resulting in ..."

"I get the picture, Captain," Veecey said. Unlike his Candorian aide, the general did have an internal filter and, as a result, did *not* tell her how hot it was that her bottom lip got all pouty when she did a briefing.

Veecey was also aware that Appdev's attractiveness – no matter how much it made him want to slay a dragon, swim an ocean with its body on his back, then carry it up a mountain in winter wearing only a loincloth and a buck knife, just to lay the prize at her feet – didn't change the fact that people were counting on him.

To snap himself back into reality, he rested his eyes on the autographed hologram of a grinning Sajak Pickfour, a ubiquitous wall hanging for a Domestic general, and that was enough to turn him off.

Next to the hologram was a screen that was already playing an amateur video of the plane dropping to a hundred meters over the target, then bodies falling from the doors. That would have been gruesome enough, but these bodies were still moving, some more acrobatically than others. The less nimble ones managed to land in the vicinity of the garrison and exploded on impact. The others alternated between spreading their limbs, tumbling side-to-side and streamlining their bodies to mimic the aerodynamics of ballistic missiles. They also exploded on impact, taking out targets that were of greater value.

"We assume they have at least one asset who worked at the Hollywood garrison, because they knew just what to take out – the enlisted barracks, the communications tower, primary C-and-C," Appdev reported.

"Casualties?"

"Still being counted, Sir," Appdev said, hesitated, then continued, "but in the hundreds."

"Where did this plane come from?" the general asked. "Put another way, where did it go?"

"We don't know, Sir. It could've come from anywhere in the region. It's all desert; even after centuries, things don't rust out there. All ground-based tracking systems were taken out in the attack, which kicked up enough dust to make our space-based tracking useless as well."

"Do we know anything else?"

"No, Sir."

"Well I do," Veecey said, hanging his head in his hands, sleeves rolled up past the elbows he had planted on his desk. "They found a tactic that beat us. They'll use it again."

He could not have been more wrong.

There was dancing in the streets.

Half of Palm Springs got drunk that night, but General Camille Dishinstaller declined. Yes, it was a great victory over Veecey and his storm troopers, but it cost the lives of two-hundred-eighty-eight valiant men and women.

The general did venture outside her headquarters to join the open-air party. After all, the insurgency's rank-and-file needed to know that their leader – the attack's mastermind – stood with them in triumph, as well as tragedy. Her presence was required in order to sanctify the celebration – and this remnant of the Well Regulated Militia needed the victory dance almost as much as it needed the victory.

Gunnery Sergeant Chuck-Claude Spamblocker, an elite soldier whom she knew by face even without nametags and insignias, forced a mug of amber beer into her hand. Not to insult the man, she brought it to her lips and slurped half of it down before summoning the high spirits to up-end the rest of the contents on the gunny himself. The other soldiers fell over each other laughing. Dishinstaller managed a smile.

She walked around for a few minutes, handing out 'attaboys' and pats on the back, gracious in her refusal of offers of peyote and psilocybin and, by and large, giving the impression that she was savoring the moment. But she couldn't wait to get back to her desk. She had work to do and couldn't afford the luxury of a drink.

Lieutenant Colonel Sanjay Sanchez, who had been sitting in her outer office, rose to attention as she entered.

"As you were, Sanjay."

"Thank you, Ma'am," he said. In principle, he had permission to sit right then, but an antiquated sense of chivalry kept the scar-faced veteran upright until the lady sat down first. "Brilliant tactic, General. Congratulations."

"Congratulate me when this is all over," she responded, then forced out, "but thanks."

"Ma'am, I have to report that Domestic troops have found our seven-thirty-seven. The crew escaped capture, but that was an irreplaceable piece of equipment."

"Let the space monkeys have it," Dishinstaller conceded. "It's not like we'll be able to use that plan of attack again."

"Ma'am? It was the most successful attack we've pulled off to date."

"So Veecey'll be expecting it. We'll never get another open goal like that. We got to think of something else."

"Yes, Ma'am, and we'll have to hurry."

"What do you mean, Sanjay?"

"Nobody knows where President Barber is, of course, but Emelem Cox-Arquette and his loyalists are back in business along the West Coast. At some point, they're going to try to rein us in."

"Great." Dishinstaller said, dripping irony. "All generals through history have had to fight wars whatever way the civilians told them to. Guess I was spoiled."

She didn't waste another moment mourning the impending loss of her autonomy. That half a beer she'd allowed herself was making its presence known in her bladder. But that pressure was not nearly as urgent as her need to put into action a plan it had inspired.

☆☆☆

Admiral Daytrader was hunched over his desk looking glum when his friend and colleague stepped in.

"Reit, are you ready?" Ziglar Tobaccoflack called through the open door, pantomiming a knock. "We have to brief the president in five minutes."

"I'm ready, Zig," the admiral said, as he grabbed a manila folder that was without question on its fourth use and stuffed it with thin, crisp sheets that contained more cheap wax filling than actual timber pulp. A ream of durable, bright-white bond paper was nowhere to be found anymore. "I just wish I had better news for the boss."

"The body count that bad?" Tobaccoflack asked, his practiced, glamorous façade slipping into an earnest expression of concern.

"Oh, no," Daytrader replied, as he joined the new foreign affairs advisor in the long hall that led to the president's office. "Battlefield medicine keeps getting better and better. Used to be, if we sent three million soldiers into combat, we'd have expected to get three hundred thousand back in body bags. But today we project only thirty thousand Domestic fatalities."

"That's great."

"Not really. We're projecting another two hundred and seventy thousand wounded. They're still being shot up, you see, they're just not dying. That means we have to keep paying them. Fact is, we're way over budget – in terms of both blood and treasure – and I'm just not seeing any return on investment."

Tobaccoflack stopped in mid-stride, gently tugging on Daytrader's lapel until the admiral stopped too.

"Listen very carefully, Reit," Tobaccoflack said. "Report the body count. That's your job. Tell the Boss about the medical advances but keep a positive spin on it. He wants to hear about saving lives, not about creating gimps. And whatever you do, for the sake of your own career, don't even bring up cutting-and-running on Friends Helping Friends. That's not going to happen. If you need more money, we'll find you more money."

"Yeah?" Daytrader responded, with equal parts anger and genuine curiosity at Tobaccoflack's presumption. "Where?"

☆☆☆

It started small. Two million were test-marketed on JohnDeereWorld and were an instant hit.

The design was classic – smooth, bold lines etched in patriotic primary colors. The calligraphy, created with loving care by the most esteemed graphic artist on CostcoWorld, evoked the long history and noble ideals of the Eminent Domain, and yet was easy to read at a glance.

Patriotic Domestic citizens gladly paid exorbitant prices for these. The more they spent, the larger and more ornate the decal, the greater their prestige among their neighbors. Co-workers actually competed to see who could buy the biggest, the best, the most. There were no complaints. The proceeds, after all, went to finance the war effort.

Soon, every hovercar, space transport and recycling scow from AppleWorld to JPMorganChaseCitiAmexJohn-HancockWorld had the words "Support Our Troops" in the shape of a bowed ribbon affixed to its aft section.

☆☆☆

Word of General Camille Dishinstaller's plan spread throughout half America. It would take half of America to pull it off.

They would succeed. America was a land under occupation. It could have no civilians anymore.

Everyone who heard of Dishinstaller's latest stratagem nodded approval and agreed to act in a simple act of defiance that, when performed in unison, would be magnified in a way no subjugated nation had ever used against its conquerors before.

The details, simple enough, were never written down but passed by word of mouth from neighbor to neighbor: the date and time of Operation Tank Trap.

☆☆☆

Acting President. *Acting* President. Emelem Cox-Arquette was at first flattered to be trusted with the role but, after a few weeks, he was well used to it.

This president business isn't so hard, he would tell himself as he took care of affairs of state-in-exile from behind his battered desk, in an office that exuded splendor gone to seed. *I could do this full-time.*

"Acting Mister President," a secretary called from the hall outside his improvised office in Hollywood. "You-know-who on line one."

Cox-Arquette stifled a sigh and pressed a button on his speakerphone, then choked down a last bite of burger before he had to speak.

"Wattseleh," he greeted the staticky box. "How's everything by you?"

"Miserable," President Watts Barber replied. "Had about enough of this hide-and-seek bullshit. Hold on – what's that echo? Hey, did you forget the security protocols we talked about? You don't have me on speaker, do you?"

"Of course not," Cox-Arquette told the speaker. "To what do I owe the pleasure of this call?"

"Just wanted to let you know my whereabouts, in case you were planning some action. Me and Arsenio just crossed from Oregon down into northern California. I'm not saying you and Dishy shouldn't run ops around here, just make sure they're surgical. Nothing large-scale that I could get caught up in."

"Of course, of course. Anything else?"

"Just take care of my country for me 'til I get back. Later, Uncle."

"Be well."

No sooner did Watts Barber hang up, than the secretary advised him of a call on line two.

"Dishy! How goes the struggle?" he called into the speaker.

"We're holding our own. Listen, I want to clear an operation with you. It involves the timberlands along the Coast."

"Why dontcha come on over?" he asked by way of invitation, slurping on a cherry cola.

☆☆☆

"Fuck," a disheveled President Watts Barber said, and flung his mobile phone into Meiss Lake. It skipped four times before sinking a quarter mile out.

Arsenio knew it meant trouble when he used that euphemism.

"Anything I can help with, Your Presidential Highness?"

"This is where we split up, Arsenio," the president said to his longtime personal assistant.

"Sir?"

"I just did something real stupid. I trusted somebody."

"Mister Cox-Arquette?"

"Yeah. Got a bad vibe from our talk just now. Something's up. I'm thinking he's liking the job too much. Never thought he'd sell me out!"

"I never would, Sir."

"Yeah, well, I can't take that chance now. I don't want to have to be looking over my shoulder so here's the deal: I'm heading south. You pick another direction and start walking. The faster the better. I see you again before this is all over, I shoot you. Got it?"

Arsenio, knowing it was useless and probably fatal to argue, just picked up his pack and headed east. It was a default decision. There wasn't a lot more west to go, and going north meant turning his back on Watts Barber, never a healthy thing to do.

☆☆☆

General Camille Dishinstaller hadn't worn her fatigues in months, not since the Well Regulated Militia transmogrified into the so-called insurgency. But the camouflage battle dress uniform felt right that day, the day following the successful execution of Operation Tank Trap. Wearing the uniform again made her feel like America was winning.

This renewed sense of strength came with a price though. Since the American government went underground, she had been her own boss and her unconventional yet most effective tactics would soon become the stuff of war college dissertations. But now, standing in the foyer of the landmark building that had once been

Grauman's Chinese Theater, with her staff and the remnants of the presidential retinue milling about, she had to defer to what was left of the Barber regime.

Trumpets sounded her host's arrival as Dishinstaller folded her sunglasses and stuck them in a tunic pocket. *Trumpets.*

Descending the tattered red velvet that covered the balcony staircase was the last remaining cabinet member.

"Emelem," the general said. "Good to see you again."

"Camille, Dollface, how are ya?" the Honesty Secretary called out, then rushed over to her. For a moment, she dreaded that he might try to kiss her on the cheek with a big *mmmmwwwwaaaaah*, as these Hollywood natives were wont to do. Instead, he whispered in her ear, "Sugar, they're calling me 'Acting President Cox-Arquette.' Gotta keep up appearances."

Then he straightened up and took a step back. They both stood as tall as they could, looking straight at each other.

"Of course," she said, sighed inaudibly and continued, "Acting Mister President."

"Aaah, knock it off, Sweetie," Cox-Arquette said, taking a sweeping step toward her with his arms outstretched. *"Mmmmwwwwaaaaah!"*

☆☆☆

Iman Appdev was parched. Parched and bored as she lay in her opulent Bellagio suite, the air conditioning struggling to keep pace with the desert heat.

General Veecey, such a nice old man, was in a meeting with Mister Croupier and had no further tasks for her until the following day, once she'd filed her report on the latest insurgent attack. Unknown to her, the Americans were calling it Operation Tank Trap.

The report began: 'In a coordinated attack, at least fourteen million unknown indigenous assets in the

Phoenix, Tucson, San Diego, Palm Springs, Los Angeles, San Francisco, Oakland, Reno, Carson City, Colorado Springs and Denver metropolitan areas flushed their commodes simultaneously at 0445 Mountain Time today, causing Lake Mead's water level to drop two meters,' and ended forty-one pages later.

It had been an ugly morning. No water meant no showers and no brushed teeth. It also meant that whatever a soldier had in her canteen was all she had to drink for the day.

So Appdev was parched.

She lay still in her air-conditioned bedroom at the Bellagio, one of the perks of being on the general staff. One of the perks of that perk was room service.

It had been hours since she first called the hotel desk, hours since she called a second time. With some sympathy for the overstressed American collaborator who took her calls, Appdev accepted the explanation that the bottled water was all sold out, that they were locating alternative sources of water as fast as they could and that everyone in the building had called in an order, so she simply stopped calling and waited her turn. She lay on her bed, a canopied king-size model, which was the softest thing she had ever rested upon. Although she knew that most human beings would luxuriate in a bed that soft, she also knew she wasn't made for comfort. If she were, she'd have picked a different career. That bed did nothing for her other than to make a simple soldier's back ache.

Not until late afternoon was there a knock on her door.

"Room service!" called a man's voice loudly, as if the throat and tongue behind those words were not the least bit scratchy with the dry Nevada dust.

Appdev rose, stiff, from the bed and unlatched the

door.

She knew many of the room service attendants by sight, if not by name. Happily, she noted that this time it was the good-looking one.

"Come in," she said with a gesture.

He did, without a word, crossing to a nightstand and setting down a linen-draped tray with a glass and a pitcher brimming with water. He almost didn't have time to fill the glass before Appdev grabbed it out of his hand and gulped it down greedily.

Ten seconds, fifteen seconds later, she came up for air. Her short gasp was followed by a satisfying 'Ahhhh.' The water was lukewarm, lacking ice, but there was something delightful about the way the lemon wheels added tartness.

"Let me fill you up again," the handsome, rough-shaven American offered, as he took the glass from Appdev's hand and turned his back as he poured.

"Please do," said the captain in her no-nonsense tone of voice. Her Candorian precepts of total honesty, unfettered by internal filter, compelled her to continue, "Your posterior is the closest thing to perfection I have ever seen."

Unfazed - it wasn't the first time he had heard that - Celltower turned again and handed her a refill, which she took more demurely than the first time.

"Sorry this took so long," he said. "It's been crazy today - no way to keep up with demand. Anyway, here you go: the best condensation ever to form outside an air conditioner."

"Thank you," she said, as she paused halfway through.

He smiled, showing all his teeth. She studied with interest the lines that crinkled his face as he grinned, the way they formed a border between the peaks of his cheekbones and the depths of his blue eyes.

"Your face suggests desirable genetic traits," she said. "What's your family name?"

He told her a name, any name, then took a linen napkin and made a chivalric show of dabbing a moist spot on the corner of her pouty lips.

"Pleased to meet you, Mister Nine-eleven."

"You can call me 'Porsche,' Ma'am."

"I'm Iman."

It wasn't the last Appdev would see of the man whose real name was G.Q. Celltower.

☆☆☆

"So, how's the war biz?"

"Our insurgency is gaining strength every day," General Dishinstaller told Emelem Cox-Arquette, masking her contempt for the inane question behind her oversized sunglasses.

They sat together in what had once been the theater manager's office, which now served as the very cramped seat of executive power of what was left of the Barber regime.

"Marvy," Cox-Arquette said, as he crunched on a large order of chili-cheese French fries. "Bee-tee-dubya, Tank Trap was a brilliant bit of business. The bad guys heard some scut about 'tank traps' and thought it had something to do with, you know, tanks, like in the military sense. So, Dishy, anything your constitutionally recognized and legitimate government can do for you?"

"Like what?"

"Like would you like some fries?" the acting president offered. "Have you tried the chicken stars?"

"Emel ... Acting Mister President, I need your authority to do everything necessary to win, no matter what the cost."

"Like what?"

"Like you don't want to know in advance."

"Dishy, *Bubbele*, you're making me all *verklempt*," he said in the ancient Hollywood dialect. "We're all fighting the same bunch of *gonifs*."

"And I'm not trying to get into a big *machlokes* with you," Dishinstaller said, using the Hollywood-isms she learned in high school. "But I need operational control. You want I should all the time be a *noodge*?"

"Fine. Go ahead. Be the *ganster macher*," Cox-Arquette agreed after a moment. He was beginning to wonder if he needed to fear Watts Barber anymore, and was becoming bolder. "But could I point you in a direction?"

"Direction? What kind of direction?"

"North," Cox-Arquette said. "Listen, Doll, if we're going to move the action along, we got to put this rivalry behind us and start working together."

She nodded.

☆☆☆

Following a review of new troops at the armory, Veecey and Croupier, America's military and civilian governors, strode back to Friends Helping Friends Civilize America headquarters at the Bellagio, talking shop, their security retinues buzzing around.

"Have you heard the latest about the suicide bombers?" Veecey asked.

"Is that what you're calling them?" Croupier inquired. "On the nets, they're 'smart bombs'."

"We found where the planes came from," the general said. "Southwestern Arizona. Nothing there but dust. Hard to believe that, in an atmosphere with so much water vapor, there'd be so little of it in certain sections. You can keep machinery forever in the desert down there. Not a drop of water in the air to make it rust, and no people around to stumble across it. A few low-tech sensor scramblers and nobody can spot them from space."

"Speaking of water?"

"We're bringing down what we can from the ships. And we have a procurement officer in Minneapolis through whom we can get all the water we need, providing we pay what they're asking.

"This procurement officer," Croupier joked, "any relation to Reit Daytrader?"

"His niece," Veecey replied, not joking.

☆☆☆

As G.Q. Celltower went about the business of spying on the occupation's headquarters, he had an uncomfortable degree of ambiguity to deal with. His president was nowhere to be found and might not even still be alive but, if he were alive, Watts Barber might have his own spies milling around. The incipient government-in-exile could have intelligence officers as well. As for Celltower himself, his allegiance was to Camille Dishinstaller, whom he considered the one most likely to come out on top. When all this was over, he was sure, the former Militia commander would preside over a new American regime. She was smart, capable, disciplined and seemed to lack the self-centeredness that inflated Barber and all his other top people. Celltower was hoping that wishful thinking wasn't clouding his judgment. He was, after all, betting his life.

All he knew was that he was to observe the Domestic brass's personal habits, report them in code known only to Dishinstaller's staff via Sanchez's couriers, compose daily reports handwritten on the Bellagio's gold-bordered double-thick napkins, then put those reports in a drop box - a hollowed-out ashcan near the casino's grand entrance - then wait for instructions that might or might not come.

Celltower had no idea what kind of side deals were being cut further up the chain of command, who was in on those deals, and who was left out. He just had a professional spook's intuition that there was more going on in Palm Springs and Hollywood than a man at his pay grade was ever going to find out.

He kept writing those reports.

Further instructions didn't come.

After some weeks, he noticed that his observations focused less on Sanmateo Veecey and M. Griffin Croupier VII. Instead, these dispatches obsessed over the habits of Iman Appdev, a charming woman but, from the war-fighting point of view, just a mid-level staff officer.

On one level, that was good tradecraft. Celltower had identified an asset who was close to the decision makers, yet was unobtrusive. She could be captured and, perhaps, turned.

On another level, his interest had become more than professional; also, he was sure that someone in Palm Springs was beginning to notice.

He needn't have worried.

Acting President Emelem Cox-Arquette did not, in fact, have spies at the Bellagio. But in return for granting General Camille Dishinstaller full operational control of the Well Regulated Militia, he had secured all incoming intelligence. The general had ordered her headquarters' staff in Palm Springs to forward all reports to Hollywood, unread.

This was all in flagrant disregard of President Watts Barber's last known orders. But Cox-Arquette knew where Barber was, when he guided Dishinstaller toward an assault on the northern Pacific coast and had reason to believe that Barber's directives wouldn't matter much longer.

So Celltower's reports were being forwarded to Hollywood - not that anybody there understood the code. The reports went unread and, ironically, ended up reused for their original purpose - as napkins.

Due to a breakdown in communication, Cox-Arquette himself had no idea why his napkins often had scribbles and gibberish on them. He chalked it up to war shortages and went on dabbing his mouth with data that could have ended the conflict without another lost life.

Nobody realized that G.Q. Celltower was falling in love with Iman Appdev. They also never got the single most useful datum on Domestic behavior - a singular fact to which Celltower referred on a daily basis.

LOOKING GOOD ON PAPER

The road had been called the Watts Barber Freeway until the occupation came. Since then - over a year at that point - the signs read 'Friendliness Road.' But General Camille Dishinstaller was old enough to remember when it was called Interstate 10.

It was 0830 and traffic stood at a dead standstill. That much, at least, hadn't changed. Of course, she was running late for a meeting with Acting President Emelem Cox-Arquette.

"What's the jam-up?" she demanded of a private doing her best to direct traffic. The general donned sunglasses and stepped out of her boxy SUV, which was stuck on an entrance ramp in an attempt to merge.

The private recognized Dishinstaller despite the sweatshirt and jeans the general wore when she wanted to remain inconspicuous. The private froze to attention, ignoring the crash on the median between two heavy vehicles, whose drivers were relying on her signals.

"Come on, out with it," the general said, with a hint of a chuckle. She was intent on a straight answer, not on intimidation.

"Ma'am, we're taking advantage of the overcast weather to move personnel and materiel between Hollywood and Palm Springs," the private said, "if that meets with the general's approval."

"Of course it does. It's the smart thing to do," Dishinstaller conceded, although she was clearly unhappy about being stuck in traffic. "Hold on. Overcast? My meteorological section called for clear skies all week."

☆☆☆

At the end of the longest boulevard of the Eminent Domain's capital stood the grounds of the presidential palace. Past the guard shack, past the great lawn, past the arboretum, past the grand entrance, stood the wing that served as the most important work space in the galaxy. Past the offices, past the tour routes and gift shops and press rooms, stood the inner sanctum. Beyond that lay the corridor to the president's personal suite: a guard desk, then a foyer, then a receiving room, then a staircase up to the master bedroom. Beyond that door lay a canopied bed with the amorous wifebot still sighing between the covers, an armoire with open doors revealing an endless cache of tailored suits, some on hangers and others not. Beyond that armoire was a door, half-open. Outside that door a guard stood, conspicuous, in his blue-red-gold uniform. On the inside of that door, one could see a richly-designed tiled floor, with a damp, velvety, crimson towel lying on the tiles, along with Sajak Pickfour's slippers, socks and bare calves.

"Nnnnnghhhh, rrrrrrrr," the president growled in this most private of moments. Then he said nothing, didn't even breathe for many long seconds. His face passed through pale to blue, he gasped, his face turned magenta; then, after a long, gaseous and fluxile venting sound, which defied onomatopoeia, he regained his healthy flesh tone.

"Ahhhh," he said. "Hoooboy. Ooh. That's one for the blog. Maybe not."

He reached for something, couldn't find it. He glanced furtively around the bathroom and still couldn't find it.

"Nealon?" he called out to the big guard with the constant

five o'clock shadow. "Nealon, would you come in here for a second?"

"Yes, Mister President?" the guard replied, as he entered the most secure room known to humankind.

"The Eminent Domain is the largest, most powerful sovereign nation in history."

"Yes, Mister President."

"Our gallant armed forces are the greatest bastion of freedom and liberty ever to fly a single flag."

"Without a doubt, Sir."

"Our economy is the engine of growth for the entire galaxy."

"As you say, Sir."

"So, Nealon ..."

"Yes, Mister President?"

"Why are we out of toilet paper?"

☆☆☆

"We burned down Oregon, Ma'am," the private told General Dishinstaller.

Oh yeah, the general recalled. *That was today.*

☆☆☆

Brosius Slipfall, the Pickfour administration's trade advisor, was one of the earliest and most ardent supporters of the American War, as the Friends Helping Friends adventure was becoming known.

"Whatever it costs," he told the president during a briefing in the immediate wake of When All Hell Broke Loose, "we'll make back in lower paper prices."

"No matter what happens," he told the president after the insurgency began to rage, "the Americans will never be so shortsighted as to destroy their own forests. They know as well as we do that America's nothing without paper."

"If you just give the situation a few weeks to stabilize, Mister President, you'll be amazed how dramatically paper prices will

..."

Slipfall never got a chance to finish that thought before the vacuum of space pulled his lungs out through his trachea.

☆☆☆

The private speaking to General Camille Dishinstaller was either being modest or wasn't fully informed. The Well Regulated Militia had torched not just Oregon, but millions of acres of neighboring states as well. Much of Washington and Idaho were charred beyond recognition, as was most of California, north of Redding.

Wind blew fire west to east across the once-picturesque hamlet of Dunsmuir, California. The Militia's saboteurs knew what they were doing when they combined heating oil, incendiary grenades, old-growth forests and the last week of June. The body-temperature air, combined with the utter lack of humidity, turned hundreds of crossroad towns like Dunsmuir into kindling. One cabin on the outskirts went up particularly fast because there were no actual structural studs holding it together. The drywall-and-muslin shack took barely a minute to be consumed. It had all the permanence of a theatrical set which in essence, is what it was.

Underneath, though, was a redoubtable concrete slab. In a corner of the slab was a trapdoor made of carbon steel. The door was secured with a padlocked, three-quarter-inch-thick cam-alloy chain.

Smoke drifted across the slab. The view of the charred remains of the Shasta National Forest shimmered in the heat. The door opened a crack: all the chain would allow.

A powerful explosion echoed through the otherwise still and silent valley, as the padlock shattered into component parts.

The door swung open. First to emerge from under the slab was a .38 handgun gripped firmly in an immense right hand. It was followed by a long and muscular arm. The .38 reported twice more. When the echoes died down, a head emerged.

"Arsenio!" Watts Barber's deep voice called out. In vain, he knew. "Arsenio?"

There was no reply.

The sovereign ruler of this hellscape holstered his gun and raised his hand to visor his eyes as he surveyed his realm. If smoke and convection hadn't limited his view, he'd have seen a scorched land, lined with buckled asphalt extending to the horizon in all directions.

"Damn."

The one-time university town of Chico sat at the edge of the devastation. It was in a run down bed-and-breakfast on the Esplanade there that Sanmateo Veecey set up his field headquarters.

Buildings on three sides were converted into makeshift burn units, as were the yards in between. Veecey had become accustomed to filtering out horrid smells – his office was in a casino that still reeked from hundreds of years of stale cigarettes – but in Chico his nostrils were filled with the never-to-be-forgotten stench of burnt flesh on a wholesale level.

And that was just the odor. The sight of the dying and barely living bodies he had to step over to get into the old B&B was beyond terrifying. He stared into faces that no longer had eyes to stare back at him. And he stared into eyes that were all that were left of faces.

The entire briefing he had hastily scheduled was conducted over the sometimes deafening shrieks and moans of the victims.

"How much forest went up?" Veecey asked an assortment of officers and civilian advisors standing around a map table, under the watchful eyes of his security detail. The heat lingered in the air and the corners of the paper maps curled up.

"We're still estimating, Sir," one young captain volunteered over the din outside. "But our best guess is something like twenty-five to thirty percent of America's entire timber stock."

Appdev fumbled with the stylus as she made a note to that effect in a digital notebook. Like most educated Domestic citizens, she eschewed these faddish devices, favoring tablets and clipboards. Writing on paper reinforced retention on a tactile level, as was widely known. Only morons hammered away on electronics.

But paper was becoming scarce.

"This is, what, the hundred-and-somethingth time the Americans have disrupted their own means of production?" the general asked rhetorically. "It better be the last. Appdev, I want all our intel resources focused on heading this off again. Griff, what have you got for us?"

"The death toll will also be devastating," M. Griffin Croupier VII reported, his own array of bodyguards standing post. "Friends Helping Friends will extend as much humanitarian aid as can be brought to bear. We've got field hospitals set up, grief counselors on the ground and economic development specialists on the way; which all adds up to nothing, compared with the loss."

Croupier heard Appdev sniffle and wondered if she were about to cry.

"It gets worse," Veecey said, twirling his ponytail. "I just heard from Admiral Daytrader. The president is fuming. Taking over America was supposed to mean that we'd be able to name our own price for paper. In fact, they're now rationing it back home, just like we are here. We've got to turn this around. *Now!*"

The meeting soon ended and its attendees scattered to take care of their to-dos, leaving Appdev and Croupier alone to write up their reports.

Croupier was sure now. Appdev had been crying.

"Rough day," he said, with genuine empathy.

"The worst," she replied, successful in her attempt to choke back tears. "They hate us. I understand that. I don't understand why, but I suppose if they'd invaded the Eminent Domain instead, we'd hate them."

"Makes sense."

"But that they'd do this to their own land, and their own people, just to spite us, is beyond me."

"It's a different culture. They look at everything, even human life, in unfamiliar terms."

"Did you see the fields?"

"Yes."

"I'm a soldier," Appdev said, straightening up and twisting her face into something like resolve. "I've seen combat. I've seen collateral damage and lived with what we've all had to do. But today I saw more ..."

And that's when, unaccustomed to filtering reality, she broke down.

Croupier held her as she cried, seemed to get a grip, then fell to pieces again. At last, she loosened her embrace, picked up her head and locked reddened eyes with the man who once had the president's ear.

"Thank you, Mister Croupier," Appdev said, as she straightened up and moved her hands from his back to his chest.

"Griff."

"Gr ..."

"Appdev!" Veecey called, as he strode in the door.

She came to attention with a crisp "Yessir."

"I want those reports uploaded to Vegas HQ immediately."

"On my way, Sir."

She double-timed it out of the room with only a momentary glance back at Croupier.

"She's really something, huh?" the general asked his civilian counterpart with a fraternal wink. He masked a surge of jealousy, as he attempted to confirm or disprove a potential romantic rival. He saw the gold ring on the third finger of Croupier's left hand, aware of how little that meant to so many married men.

"Yes," Croupier replied. "Who'd have guessed that under all that practiced military bearing, was such a fragile child?"

"Uh, yeah, that too. But I mean, the whole package, if you know what I mean, I mean."

Croupier was confused for a moment, then realized that Veecey was still staring at the door she'd walked out of, as if replaying her exit over again in his mind.

"Oh, I wouldn't know about that, Mat."

"Come on, it's just us here. Admit it. She's one tight little unit."

"Well, Mat, I guess you hadn't heard," Croupier said, with demure delicacy. "I'm from PradaWorld."

"Oh," the general replied.

And that was nowhere near enough of a verbal cue for Croupier to infer whether or not Veecey knew what that meant.

☆☆☆

"You're late," Cox-Arquette said by way of greeting, as Camille Dishinstaller entered his confined office.

"Traffic," she replied. "I brought burgers."

"Then all's forgiven. Except for the we're-not-winning-the-war thing."

"Not yet," the general allowed. "Disrupting their supply of paper has got to be hurting them, though."

"Apparently, not enough," the acting president said. "We got to find a way to hit them in those deep pockets of theirs."

"Look, you tell me to kill somebody, I'll kill him. You tell me to blow something up, it'll be gone by morning. But economic warfare isn't what I was trained for."

"Honey, all I knew how to do after college was write press releases," the acting president said. "Let's think. Where are they coming up with the money? Income taxes? Sales taxes? Special usage fees?"

"Magnetic ribbons."

"Right. I heard about those," Cox-Arquette said pensively. "How much are they selling for?"

☆☆☆

There were no direct trade links between America and the Eminent Domain. But still.

Emelem Cox-Arquette had a brother-in-law with an import-export business. The brother-in-law had a neighbor with a factory that took advantage of the cheap labor to be had in Sweden. The neighbor had a cousin who lived among the American expatriate community on PanasonicWorld, where he worked as a customs inspector and whose discretion could be relied upon.

Within the week, knock off Support Our Troops ribbons were being sold to patriotic citizens throughout the Eminent Domain for half price.

The proceeds, being deposited in a bank account in a Kleptocosm outworld, were then repatriated through two other money-laundering havens before ending up in a bank across the street from an arms merchant in Ensenada. That Baja California port had, for a dozen years or more, been firmly under control of Mexico, America's historical rival, but recent events being what they were, Mexican sentiment had been warming to the American cause.

The money bought weaponry, ammunition and food for the Well Regulated Militia and America's government-in-hiding. It also paid for hired mercenaries from other Earth nations and, eventually, from Grand Organ members throughout the civilized galaxy. The result was more forests in flames, more Domestic troops being measured for prosthetics.

President Pickfour, out of necessity, had to go on the galacticam and exhort people to 'Support our troops by not buying ribbons that say 'Support Our Troops'.'

☆☆☆

"C'mon, admit it," President – as he now insisted – Emelem

Cox-Arquette chided General Camille Dishinstaller, once again his guest at his Hollywood office.

"Fine," she replied. "OK."

"That's not admitting it, Doll. Where's the love, Dishy?"

"That was brilliant, Mister President," she conceded in a singsong voice. "You are a master tactician."

He leaned back in his chair and gobbled a handful of chili-cheese fries in celebration.

"So you'll stick to the soldiering and leave the rest to Uncle?"

"Yes, Mister President," she said, still standing in her beloved fatigues.

"Good girl, good girl. Look, I want you to transfer your spies to civilian control ... we can move faster as we find out more about these *shmucks*."

"You've been getting their reports. I haven't seen anything new from them in months."

"Yeah ... but they still think they're reporting to you ... I get the feeling they also think we're working against each other. With our dear leader presumed barbecued, it's important that you and me show a united leadership."

She respected the chain of command. She also respected, albeit not as much, Watts Barber. She respected Emelem Cox-Arquette even less. Overriding all of that, however, was her desire to keep her troops focused on the fight against the common enemy. And her love for America.

"Yes, Mister President."

Hours later she was back in Palm Springs, directing Lieutenant Colonel Sanjay Sanchez to inform all intelligence officers that they were now under the direct command of America's new, self-appointed president.

☆☆☆

'im like so totaly into Brandon ☺' GoWildcats97792 tapped into the chatroom window.

Message for me, America's inside man at Friends Helping Friends headquarters decoded, as he tapped away on the keyboard of the ancient desktop in a Bellagio sub-basement. *Finally!*

'hes a QT!!!!!' G.Q. Celltower entered in. *I read you.*

'it was like really freezing in bio class yesterday and he was like sure you can wear my letter jacket.'

Intelligence operations are hereby transferred to civilian control by order of General Dishinstaller. Extend all courtesy to President Cox-Arquette or his designees.

Celltower glanced at the screen in disbelief.

'you are such a rock star! boys in my school stick straws up their nostrils to get attention'

Please repeat transmission.

'it was like really freezing ...'

That was that. These orders were being transmitted by GoWildcats97792, the unique call sign for Gates Branchmanager, Colonel Sanjay Sanchez's communications officer. If it came through Sanchez, then it started with Dishinstaller. End of discussion. These were orders.

☆☆☆

Most Domestic citizens in Pickfour's time couldn't tell you who President Giselle Desksergeant was. Under her long-ago stewardship, the Eminent Domain was tranquil in its borders, its people happy, so she had been forgotten with ease. Anyone who ever toured the presidential palace though, knew the Desksergeant Room, so named the day of her state funeral. It was grandly furnished with rare artifacts presented by visiting dignitaries and heads of state from a thousand systems. It wasn't just the official waiting room for the president's outer office, not just a room in which a dozen presidents had called informal staff discussions during hundreds of crises, it was a museum testifying to how far the human race had come. It was filled with plaster casts of first footprints on new worlds, actual instrumentation from all the galaxy's most legendary pioneering spacecraft, as well as tantalizing relics from alien cultures which had died out millions of years before. In hushed tones, people spoke in awe of the Desksergeant Room's treasures or, as President Pickfour famously called them, *doohickies.*

Suddenly, there was one fewer. Pickfour had spilled coffee on the exoskeletal remains of one of the original, water-soluble life forms of WachoviaWorld. It fizzled away in clouds of oxygen and methane.

"Heidi, clean this up – and open a window," President Pickfour demanded, the methane smell inside more of a concern than the steady drizzle outside. "Now, Smokey, will you explain this to me?"

"The polls show that the Loyal Opposition has been gaining ground, making an issue out of your handling of the war," said Ziglar Tobaccoflack, newly elevated to Croupier's old post and wearing a new sequined suit for the occasion.

"As if they could do any better," the president replied. "But I still don't understand these polls."

"Well, you still have a fifty-three percent approval rating, but twenty-nine percent of the Domestic population disapproves, and eighteen percent are undecided. That contrasts with last week's ..."

"Let's not dwell on ancient history. Tell me again about this week."

Tobaccoflack smiled through it all, relying on all his theatrical training to suppress just how flustered he was.

Still, the one-time galacticam star could feel the sweat forming in every pore. How would Griff Croupier handle this, he wondered. It didn't help. Nor did wondering why the president insisted on calling him 'Smokey.' He soon realized it was especially unhelpful to wonder, *What's the last thing a depressurized body feels before it explodes in space?*

"Oh, by the way – been meaning to tell you," the president continued. "Nice suit."

Tobaccoflack felt as if his face were bathed in sunlight

shining through suddenly parted clouds, as a heavenly choir sang wordless melodies, accompanied by a thousand strings.

"You see, Mister President, there are a hundred people out there and they're each named Percent ... "

Tobaccoflack proved better than his predecessor at explaining things to Sajak Pickfour. Within the hour, he had succeeded in expressing that the American insurgency was stepping down its attempts at deforestation. That was because Veecey's staff had made anti-deforestation its major priority. The bad news was that attacks on Domestic soldiers were on the rise because all intel resources, dedicated to protecting the troops, had been pulled off to deal with protecting the trees.

"Then put those resources back to work preventing attacks on our own people," the president directed.

"It shall be done, Sir," Tobaccoflack replied.

And the forests were soon ablaze once more.

☆☆☆

Paper was becoming scarce at the Bellagio, so Sanmateo Veecey had ceased his practice of making paper copies of the image in Iman Appdev's personnel file. Instead, he had it downloaded into a handheld device, stored in liquid crystal in a frame on his nightstand and projected on the metre wide screen at the foot of his bed.

On one typical night, he lay in bed naked, his uniform hanging stiffly in the wardrobe, surrounded by electronic pictures of Iman Appdev's face illuminated by the candlelight of a dozen hazelnut-scented votives, while a perfect, equalized and noise-squelched sequence of Luther Vandross classics played softly from his custom sound system.

He wondered if anyone knew about his fascination for her. He had, after all, arranged for three men, whom he suspected of having their attentions reciprocated, to be transferred to Iowa; he hoped that wasn't too much of a clue. There was a lot of fighting out there on the Plains and tens of thousands of Veecey's officers and troops received similar orders from him.

He decided it was safe to continue with that maneuver.

There was still one potential rival, though - one man whom he couldn't put in the line of fire with one word.

Griff Croupier.

Was he interested in Appdev? Veecey honestly wasn't sure. He recalled that Croupier was married, but Veecey couldn't decide if it mattered that he was. Veecey figured he'd keep an eye on Croupier, just to monitor the situation.

Asking Croupier flat out about his intentions was out of the question. Veecey had his own secrets when it came to his sex life; something like professional courtesy proscribed him from asking about anyone else's.

Veecey was hoping nothing would come of it. He liked Croupier who was, after all, a likeable man by profession. Croupier was also the only one he could talk to on the entire planet, with whom rank or nationality didn't come into play. He would hate to lose the only person he could converse with.

He drifted off to sleep. His last semi-conscious thoughts were not about Appdev, though, nor were they about Croupier. They were about Vandross. How there was something less than authentic about what he was hearing. How that silky voice was meant to be heard over the occasional intrusion of static or popping ...

After days of wandering, wooly hair growing out in odd clumps, Watts Barber was home.

Sacramento.

It wasn't where he was born and it wasn't where he grew up. It was where he first rose to fame and, some time later, to power. It was a city that valued his ball-handling skills, true; it was also, by happy coincidence, the city that became America's capital in the wake of the Eastern Seaboard disaster, which later generations referred to only as That Thing We Don't Talk About. In short, it was a city made for a ruthless, power-mad sociopath with delusions of grandeur and a flawless three-pointer. It was in Sacramento that Watts Barber lived the American Dream.

Now it overflowed with refugees, beggars and crying children.

Here, he could be anonymous.

☆☆☆

"There are too many of them," General Sanmateo Veecey said to his civilian counterpart and only real friend, as they huddled in a small meeting room off the Bellagio's main gaming hall.

It smelled in the room. The thick cigarette smell endemic in casinos was the least of it.

People from the Eminent Domain were fond of water. They drank it in huge quantities. The privileged classes prided themselves on their palates for exotic mineral blends, fruit juice traces and novel distillation processes. But Earth's gravity played havoc with their reflexes. The origin planet had gained just a little in density in the centuries since humanity took to the stars and thus Earth had a slightly stronger gravitational pull than the standard to which the Eminent Domain's artificial worlds were constructed. It was deceptively close to that standard though. The Domestic troops weren't gasping for breath or crushed under the burden.

They were, however, clumsy. They spilled as much water as they consumed. Mold was growing everywhere as the carpets grew lumps and the wallpaper curled.

"And there's more of them and their sympathizers every day," M. Griffin Croupier VII agreed, pouring himself a glass of water, and then some.

"Any chance of getting more troops?"

"No," was all Croupier could say to that.

"I didn't want to go this route ... but it looks like losing an arm or leg isn't an automatic ticket home anymore," Veecey said, with a heavy shrug.

Croupier kept to himself any hopeful comment about how

wondrous the medical advances had been as a result of this war.

"You know what we have to do, don't you?" Veecey asked.

Croupier had an idea where Veecey was headed.

"We have to raise an indigenous army," the general continued.

Croupier decided not to add his ironic observation that he hoped it would be as good as the indigenous army they were already fighting.

"We need another million troops on the ground here," Veecey concluded. "We're liberators, right? Most Americans are happy to see us? It's time they showed some gratitude and got their own damn bandits under control."

"I agree, Mat, but if you take that step, others follow," Croupier ended his silence by saying. "Unless you're proposing an American corps as part of the Domestic military, then we need a new American government for them to swear allegiance to. Any chance we can co-opt the government-in-hiding?"

"It's not like we haven't been looking," Veecey countered. "They're somewhere in or around Hollywood, we just don't know where. Every time one of our intel people gets anywhere close, someone spots them at once and tips off any Barber henchmen who might be around. Then they scatter before we can call in reinforcements."

"Tips them off how?"

"They have a code word for 'Friends Helping Friends military personnel.' They call us *shmucks*. It's the one Hollywoodese term we've been able to decipher."

"Might not be worth the effort to negotiate with them anyway," Croupier conceded. "These are Barber's handpicked people. They've got to be hardcore."

"Any other places we can look for new leadership?"

"Not really. The ethnic Americans living in the Eminent Domain haven't demonstrated any interest in coming back to live."

"I noticed they haven't demonstrated any interest in coming back to serve in uniform. So what we're saying then ..." the general began.

"... we have to build a nation from the ground up."

☆☆☆

Watts Barber, his trademark angular pate obscured by clumps of tight curls, sat down on a picnic bench overlooking his cherished Sacramento.

He wasn't in Sacramento per se, but in Natomas Park across the river – the American river. He stared at the ruins of the office buildings that once housed the California state bureaucracy, back in the days when there were states and bureaucracies and offices. Long before Barber sat down that day to swallow his traditional American breakfast of a cheese burrito and watery beer, the Richards Boulevard section north of downtown Sacramento had become as overgrown as the park.

Natomas Park, incidentally, was swarming with Domestic troops, which didn't worry Watts Barber. They weren't looking for him. They were looking for trees.

Since the fire that destroyed most of the timberland to the north, the Domestic military was scouring every glade and arbor for its paper quota. Between lumberjacking and training Americans how to kill their trainers, Domestic troops hardly did any fighting anymore. They had subcontractors for that.

The photon-saws the troops used were near-silent tree fellers. There was no buzzing as there was from the indigenous, combustion-driven American tools. The only sound was the thunderous crash of tumbling redwoods. The Domestics knew they were supposed to yell 'Timber!' at some point in the process but, whoever wrote the procedural manual had obviously been confused and, as a result, the cadence went: *sssszt, crack, thump*, 'Timber!'

Barber had seen the results before. Just the day before, in the same park, he saw a family of three die, in a most horrid manner, that way. Their own fault, Barber reasoned, they should have been paying attention. That morning, as Barber was swallowing his last swig of beer, it was a low-level Domestic soldier who found himself crushed under a tree, not fifty feet from where he himself sat.

"Oh no!" shouted a Domestic voice. "They killed Coder!"

"Bastards!" came a comrade's reply.

Barber sat there, detached and dispassionate, not caring about the latest fatality and with enough confidence in his own agility and reaction time to not worry about himself.

Suddenly, the action stopped.

Barber didn't think for a minute it was out of respect or concern for the fallen soldier. Barber was still interested in knowing the reason why the clear-cutting of Natomas Park had paused, out of boredom more than anything else.

He noticed two Friends Helping Friends officers arguing. One was in the uniform of another space-borne civilization allied to the Eminent Domain.

"We didn't sign up for this!" the officer who wore the uniform of the Associated Market shouted.

That was the only part of the conversation Barber could make out for a while, as the Market officer regained his military bearing and the rest was conducted in hushed tones. Still, there were some animated hand gestures.

Barber tried to guess what the argument was about. Nobody - not in the Eminent Domain, not in the Associated Market, not even in America - really cared about trees. Nor did he believe anyone of any importance cared about the human body count on either side. Maybe he was just judging everyone else by his own standards.

Abruptly, the hand gestures became finger pointing, with the Market officer pointing up high, into a tree limb. The Domestic officer squinted, as the object the Market officer was indicating was right at the edge of his vision. Barber could see it plainly though: a seagull.

"Don't you know they're endangered?" Barber heard the Market officer ask snootily.

Ennui alone doesn't explain why Watts Barber picked that moment to take the antique .38 pistol out of its leg holster, line up with the bird and fire a single shot, straight through the belly of his target. He was bored, true, and it was a momentary distraction. He also hadn't killed anyone, or anything, in a while and missed the stimulation. And he was cognizant that he was blessed with one particular talent – nigh-on superhuman eye-hand coordination – and that this blessing was a strictly use-it-or-lose-it proposition and he needed to keep in practice.

But most of all, Watts Barber had been sleeping in cellars and caves and abandoned buildings. For months. He was simply tired of running.

"Thanks!" shouted the Domestic officer, to his colleague's chagrin.

The troops went back to work. Three more trees fell. Four.

Then it occurred to the Domestic officer: Only one man on the planet had aim like that.

☆☆☆

"America used to be a much larger country," Veecey said, as he poured Croupier another ice water back at Friends Helping Friends headquarters in Las Vegas. They were making small talk and watching the sunset from what was once Watts Barber's private suite, as it had become their routine, putting the carnage at Chico behind them as best they could.

"Thanks. What happened?" Croupier asked in response. From his seat in a lounge chair on a penthouse balcony of the erstwhile Bellagio, he could see the whole town. He could also see the sun setting, behind pillars of smoke, on the western horizon but chose not to focus on those.

"According to American folklore, the entire northeast quarter just died out in a single generation. It just ran out of children."

"How did that happen?"

"It's widely believed that the Northeasterners made

homosexuality mandatory."

"Come on. That's not even possible," Croupier said, wondering if Veecey would ask about his credentials to make such a claim.

"According to the ancient tales, anyone who wasn't homosexual was required to have abortions," Veecey continued.

Croupier kept wondering if Veecey was even aware of PradaWorld's most definitive institution.

"People really believe this?" Croupier asked.

"I don't," said Veecey. "But I'm just a simple soldier and history buff. Who am I to stand between a nation and its founding myths?"

"According to my briefing papers, you're more than just a 'buff' Mat," Croupier recalled, showing off that he had read up on his colleague. "With your background, don't you want to know what really happened to New York?"

"Yeah," Veecey said, with a pervasive wistfulness. "When all this is over, I'd like to join a dig in Manhattan - find out what happened to Carnegie Hall, the Apollo, Lincoln Center."

"You know, Nashville is still a thriving city ... and under our control. You could always ..."

"Thanks, Griff, but I studied *music* history. Now let's get back to business. Tobaccoflack thinks the president is going to want to inspect the troops first hand - show the voters back home he's ..."

"Excuse me, Sirs," Appdev said, shy, as she stepped out on the balcony.

"Hi, Iman," Croupier said. "How are you this morning?"

"Fine, Gri... Sir, thanks. General - it's unconfirmed - but a unit attached to the Sacramento command thinks it has Watts Barber in custody."

"How sure are we?" Veecey asked.

"The company commander seems quite certain, Sir."

"That's great news! Outstanding!" Veecey said, loud enough

to hear his voice echo off the distant canyon walls.

"Yes, thank you so much, Captain," Croupier said.

"My pleasure, Sir," she replied, smiled at Croupier, then turned to Veecey, all business.

"Dismissed," Veecey said after a moment.

"Well, Mat, you want to call the president?"

"Hmm? No, I want to make certain first. Why don't you go ahead and call Tobaccoflack though?"

"Sure thing. We'll talk about the president's trip later."

"Oh yeah, sure. Later," the general muttered as Croupier entered his suite and rushed straight to the comnet console.

In one compartment of his mind, General Sanmateo Veecey was running through the protocol of checking the identity of the Sacramento prisoner, keeping a lid on it, notifying President Pickfour, making announcements to the media, before handing him off to the intelligence service.

In another, he was marveling at the beauty of the American desert at twilight. So many colors, so many layers, so much untamed majesty.

And no one to share it with him. Appdev was the only woman who interested Veecey and she was clearly more interested in that civilian fop Croupier. And, unless he was sorely mistaken and had totally misjudged the situation - and you don't get to be a general by making mistakes in judgment, so he was very certain he was right about this - Croupier was out to steal her away.

☆☆☆

Iman Appdev shrieked and, at first, G.Q. Celltower couldn't tell if it was out of pain or delight.

She grabbed her temples as she fell off her bed and onto her knees.

After a minute, she regained her feet.

"What was that?" Appdev asked the handsome man from room service. He stood by attentively as she composed herself, sitting at the foot of her canopied bed, hoping her superiors would forgive her some afternoon slacking.

"Brain freeze," Celltower said.

"That had quite a kick," she said with a gasp. "What was it you called it?"

"A Slurpee, Ma'am."

He had to admit that he was really enjoying his job. He was doing his patriotic duty by turning a member of Veecey's staff into an intelligence asset, but he was giddy beyond belief at the prospect of spending so much time in a hotel room with her. He would seduce her, he knew, but that would have to wait until she thought it was her idea.

"It's divine. How do you make one? Never mind, I don't want to know," she said, then took one last, appreciative, sip and lay back on the supple mattress. "Just bring another tomorrow."

"Whatever you like, Ma'am," he said. "If you like, I could also introduce you to the pleasure that is Krispy Kreme."

Her expression changed in a blink. A man who wasn't aware of Eminent Domain mores might have been puzzled. Not Celltower.

"Get out."

"I didn't mean to offend ..." he spluttered, feigning surprise at her reaction.

"Get out!"

He did.

She's not ready, he thought. *I didn't think she was but I had to know for sure.*

Soon, though.

It was true. General Sanmateo Veecey confirmed it via comnet chat with the Sacramento base commander. DNA confirmed it. Watts Barber had been captured.

Veecey ordered the deposed American president to be taken, under heavy guard, to the Southern Desert Correctional

Facility, west of Las Vegas. He then conferenced in the commandant of the prison.

"He's not to be tortured," the general ordered. "He's not even to be interrogated. Either he's really been on the run all this time and has no idea how the insurgency operates, or else he's allowed himself to be captured for his own reasons and we can't trust a thing he says."

Veecey had no way of knowing for certain that he was right on both counts.

M. Griffin Croupier VII had very low expectations.

Building a new American army was a ridiculous assignment to start with he pondered, as he sat hunched over the desk in his suite in the Bellagio. The first thing the Domestic military did was dissolve and disarm the Well Regulated Militia - at least as far as was known at the time. It had become apparent that there was still quite a large corps out there in Hollywood. Croupier was more frightened, though, by how quiet things had been on the Plains.

There was a knock on the door and Croupier jumped up to race over to it. Regaining his cool, he stood at the bolted door for a count of three, then unlatched it. It was Major G.Q. Celltower of the Well Regulated Militia or, as Croupier knew him, Porsche, the room service boy with the great tushy.

"Good evening, Mister Croupier," the spy said. "Your consommé and Virgin Mary."

"Good evening, Porsche - just set the tray down on the nightstand."

"Very good, Sir. My, you've been ordering up a lot of late."

"Wish I could chat a little ... but I'm just swamped with work," he said, giving Celltower a tip that revealed much about how well the livery pants were fitting that night.

"Anything I can do to help?"

"Not unless you want to join the new American army we're forming to take over once we leave," Croupier said.

"Why, I'd be delighted to, Sir."

"That's sweet," Croupier replied. "Are there a few million more like you?"

"Certainly are, Sir," Celltower said, sensing an opportunity and thinking on his feet. "You just have to reach them through the netcasts."

"Commercials?"

"Yessir! Here in America, advertising is a sacrament," Celltower continued. "Producing them means making the pilgrimage to Hollywood, our holy city."

"Sounds dangerous."

"We're a peace-loving people," Celltower said with such sincerity, that Croupier forgot that he was referring to precisely those people with whom he was at war and trying to recruit as his own paid mercenaries. "I have a friend who can show you around."

A solemn shadow filtered across Celltower's dazzling eyes, then suddenly dropped. Croupier, who was too busy deciding if those eyes were more of a steel blue or a robin's-egg blue, failed to notice any signs of epiphany behind them. He did decide, however, that the man's eye color was a factor of the lighting and in the incandescence of the hotel suite, it was steel blue. Definitely steel blue. Irresistible steel blue.

Celltower went on to tell Croupier more about Hollywood, but all Croupier could remember was something about 'music history' and 'important' and 'music history.' Croupier was certain that the man's eyes would be robin's-egg blue in the hazy Hollywood sun. He fantasized about being a pair of Ray-Bans.

Celltower left, his job done and his tip generous in the extreme.

Croupier direct-dialed Veecey's suite.

"Mat, hi ... I'm going to Hollywood tomorrow for a meeting that might solve our local recruitment problem. Care to come with?"

M. Griffin Croupier VII and General Sanmateo Veecey left for Hollywood the next morning, packed in a fossil-fueled van crammed together with their security detail. With all that firepower around, Croupier didn't fear for his own safety. He did, however, fear making a decision as bad as those Thierstein or Slipfall had made.

He also wondered why Veecey seemed so irritable. Croupier thought they were becoming friends, which would be enough to make Steve jealous, if he were there with them. Croupier realized how much he missed his husband. And wondered why messages from back home were less and less frequent.

Tinted shatterproof windows capped the heavily armored sedan. The bodyguard behind the steering wheel took them down Hollywood Boulevard, varying speeds to discourage sniper fire. Just as she jackrabbit-accelerated across Gower Street, Veecey pressed his face against a window and ordered, "Stop the van!"

Preceded and followed by his guards, the Domestic general emerged from a rear door and lifted his face to the sky. His face was illuminated with something resembling religious devotion.

"Leave me here, Griff," he told his civilian counterpart. "Pick me up when you're done."

Croupier paused a moment out of concern for Veecey, before closing the door and ordering the driver to go.

The van sped off. Four nervous guards surrounded Veecey, waving the barrels of their weapons in all directions, at random. In an effort to anticipate his movements, they kept a tight circle around him as, unhurried, he approached Vine Street.

Sanmateo Veecey found himself on hallowed ground. He resisted the temptation to drop to his knees as he looked up thirteen stories to behold, in all its glory, the Capitol Records

Building.

Croupier and the rest of the security retinue proceeded the kilometer and a half west to his appointment.

The room service boy's friend turned out to be very helpful. The paunchy old man told Croupier he had been a producer of commercials 'back in the day,' and was grateful that Porsche, whom he described with affection, as *'mein boychick,'* would think to send such an important man his way.

The man, who had an office in an abandoned motion picture theater, gave his name as Fleetwood Brougham.

☆☆☆

Surrounded by bodyguards, General Sanmateo Veecey approached the circular building, reminiscent of a stack of records on an antique turntable.

Before entering the building, he knelt down and, *pianissimo,* kissed John Lennon's star, still bright and shining centuries after its emplacement.

Another stride took him past the star engraved to pedal-steel pop star Garth Brooks. The majesty of the earlier moment gave Veecey the strength he needed to overcome the urge to pee.

He and his guards crossed the threshold into the lobby.

The once grand entrance had been abandoned in haste. Veecey couldn't tell if the evacuation took place that morning, or the day of the invasion – two years ago already! – or before Watts Barber even came to power. Maybe it was before Barber or Veecey had even been born.

It was immaterial. The lobby was strewn with trash. Veecey, with morbid curiosity sorted through the rubbish. He picked up what he knew from texts to be a 45rpm single. Taking it gingerly out of its dust jacket, holding it as if it was the finest bone china, he read the label: 'For Airplay Only/Les Paul and Mary Ford/How High the Moon.'

There were rotting cartons all over the place. Who knew

how many of these treasures were being left to the elements, or the Southern Californian equivalent? It wasn't looting, per se. It was preserving.

"Kilborn," he called out, *appassionato*, to the nearest bodyguard. "Get some crates. And another van."

☆☆☆

In the haze of days and nights Croupier spent in meetings with Brougham and his staff, Veecey called on the comnet to say something about getting his own ride back and Croupier had said 'Sure no problem.'

Croupier couldn't believe how much was involved in a media blitz. He also couldn't believe how much it cost. Nor could he believe what these people ingested.

But several small fortunes later, the commercials were on the netcasts and the results were astonishing. Croupier mused that, considering the flood of recruits who showed up at the Domestic training camps, he could have met his quota spending only a tenth of what he paid Brougham.

Forthwith, almost as if they were already obeying orders to join, the recruits flooded in. Were some of these people the same ones they disarmed two years ago? Without doubt. They had captured and released so many prisoners back then, who could keep up?

According to General Veecey's training specialists, these recruits had the makings of good troops, albeit slow to learn. It confounded the Domestic military that it took so long to turn them into soldiers. Financial incentives were agreed upon but, for some reason, the more Friends Helping Friends paid the American trainees each month, the more months it took for them to complete their training.

In the end, though, these Americans in their new uniforms were far better armed than they were when hostilities first broke out.

Most, but by no means all, were from California and Nevada. Many were from the Plains.

It lasted longer than his recruitment budget but soon, Croupier's training budget was spent.

And, all of a sudden, desertion was becoming a problem.

Perhaps, if General Sanmateo Veecey had given the disruption his full attention, he could have prevented the American volunteers from drifting back to the insurgency. He could have, possibly, also prevented a large proportion of them from joining the Terrahists. But he was content to let his civilian counterpart handle it all.

Since returning from the Capitol Records Building, he had little time for anything besides the stack of vinyl recordings he found there. Miraculously, it seemed, he also found an ancient Technics turntable in the wrecked lobby - in perfect working condition.

Veecey had learned in school about the richness, the texture of music recorded on vinyl. He hadn't believed it until he experienced it himself, though. He was, *allegro y giocoso,* hooked.

He slept less and less, becoming more and more distracted. His own troops noticed the change.

So did his enemies.

MANNA

I can't believe they're still here," President Emelem
Cox-Arquette complained, storming around his office at
Grauman's Chinese Theater. "They're broke. They're
hated by the people they're trying to help. I hear the
rest of the galaxy thinks they've gone off their rockers.
What does it take to get these *shmucks* to declare
victory and go home?"

"Again, this isn't exactly my area of expertise,"
Dishinstaller prefaced, "but we need to eat at their troop
morale."

"Yeah, these Domestic *boychicks* can really take a
beating. Something's got to get to them, though."

"The harder we hit them, the tougher they think they
are and the more they want to stick it out," Dishinstaller
said. "We don't have the military capacity to deal them
the kind of blow that would make them turn tail."

"Something's got to irritate them," America's acting
president said, between bites of cheesy-crust pizza.
"Think. If you were one of Pickfour's goons, what kind
of *tsuris* would you have?"

"I'm kind of at the end of my Hollywoodese,"
Dishinstaller admitted, grabbing a slice of pizza for
herself. It was still hot, a little too hot. "Is there a

Nebraskan synonym for *tsuris*?"

"Not strictly, no," Cox-Arquette said. "I'm asking, 'If you were on the other side, what would be eating your heart out?' "

She paused in thought. There was an uncomfortable silence. Then she felt the sensation of either tomato sauce or molten magma dropping on her wrist. She grabbed a napkin off the acting president's desk noting, casually at first, that the gold-trimmed napkin had the Friends Helping Friends logo on it – and a sketch of the Bellagio.

"Emelem, where did you get this?"

"Mom-and-pop pizza place about four blocks over. They deliver."

"No, the napkin."

"I don't know what's up with that. We get a stack of napkins from Vegas every day."

She turned over the napkin in her hand and read the contents, translating the code in her head as best she could.

"Emelem, this is from my inside guy."

"Celltower? Yeah, I know him," Cox-Arquette said. "He sent that Croupier *feygele* our way."

"Right. He's a quick thinker – made the right move there and got us quite a stockpile."

"Plenty of cash too. What's *mein boychick* been up to?"

"Don't know. We'd lost touch a couple of weeks ago. I didn't want to initiate contact in case he was under deep cover but ... if I read this right ..."

Dishinstaller pulled out her secure field phone and hit a speed-dial button.

"Major?" she inquired, stepping into the hall so she could stretch. "Dishinstaller here, with President Cox-Arquette. You probably think this is an obvious question but we've had some, uh, cryptographic problems. What do Domestic troops eat? ... Do they? ... Really? ... That's fascinating. Thank you, *Colonel* Celltower."

She stepped back into Cox-Arquette's office.

"Mister President," she announced, "we will now win us the war."

She explained what she meant and suddenly it made sense to Cox-Arquette. He wondered why he hadn't figured it out for himself. Of course, the only Domestic citizen he'd ever met was M. Griffin Croupier in his guise as Fleetwood Brougham.

But it all dovetailed.

☆☆☆

Sajak Pickfour had been president for only a few months when All Hell Broke Loose. Before that, he was an affable, popular, but not very accomplished, regional satrap who was realistic enough to dream about the presidency without any illusion that he could ever attain it.

But that was before the gas attack.

Justin Jeopardy, a gregarious man who seemed to never miss a chance to be in a room with three hundred other people wanting to shake his hand, had been an immensely popular president. The worlds were at peace. Trade was ascendant. Wealth was transcendent. And the Eminent Domain's cultural influence, political suasion and military standing were unrivaled throughout the Milky Way.

Then, one day, while he was in the middle of a speech in the Hall of All Opinions, a tiny hiss was heard coming from the podium. He ploughed on, assuming nobody heard it. But every engineer recording the event knew that sound. It would have been enough to convict him had they chosen to ignore it, which they might have. But the hiss was followed by a ripping sound, audible to everyone in attendance and to billions tuning in at home. The ripping was, in turn, followed by three gurgles of decreasing volume. There could be no question about it. His Excellency, President Justin Jeopardy, WholesaleLiquidatorsWorld's favorite son had, very publicly, farted.

He tried to deny it. His handlers went right to work on the spin: He didn't do it, but if he did, could you blame him? And if you could blame him, was it really so bad an offense as to outweigh all the peace and prosperity the people had enjoyed under his tenure? And if it really was so bad, was it any worse than anything other public officials had done? And if it were worse, did it really sink below the deeds of the typical citizen who came up, as President Jeopardy himself did, through humble and humbling circumstances?

Well, yes it did, his critics – of which all of a sudden there were many – said. The president was expected to behave with a certain amount of decorum. Since the advent of deep space travel, people had eaten manna (originally a capital M brand name but which for a century had been rendered in lower case), referring to any of a number of widely available nutrition bars which had the added convenience of being fully metabolized and produced no biological waste. This manna had been a boon to humanity, which had traveled in cramped circumstances and often settled in them as well. People needed to eat but they didn't have room to dispose of their solid wastes, so they ate manna. People became creative with it and added new flavors and textures and even developed a form that eliminated the need to urinate as well. Nobody in decent society, certainly not a head of state, had reason to have such a rude biological reaction.

So why did he do it? To the nation's discredit,

nobody for a moment wondered if the president might be ill. They cut right to the chase: "What has Gustin' Justin been eating?"

At first President Jeopardy's handlers said it was an exotic food some other Grand Organ dignitary had offered him, which would have been impolite to decline. None of these dignitaries stepped forward to take any share of the blame, which was enough for the president's enemies in the Archsenate to go to work on him. They appointed a special prosecutor, gave him unlimited funding and staffing and empowered him to use zealous means that would never be permitted in most jurisdictions.

Years and fortunes later, the prosecutor reported back to the Archsenate. Justin Jeopardy did willingly and with premeditation consume thirty-eight grams of a substance known as scrapple.

"What is scrapple?" the chairwoman of the Archsenate Special Subcommittee on Presidential Flatulence inquired.

"It comes from a pig. Does the subcommittee ..." the prosecutor began.

"The subcommittee, being comprised in part by representatives from terraformed agricultural colonies, knows what pigs were."

"Begging Madam Chairwoman's pardon, but what pigs *are*."

"We were under the impression they were extinct, since their only purpose was as human feed – a need long since filled by manna," she said after a brief caucus with her colleagues.

"They are still raised as pets on some obscure worlds, even – and it pains me to say this – kept as livestock on others."

A gasp rippled through the hall.

"Order!" the chairwoman directed and, in short order, the crowd hushed. "How did President Jeopardy come into possession of a pig?"

"He didn't, Madam Chairwoman, but he did come into possession of a product extracted from pigs: scrapple."

"Mister Prosecutor, I've heard of pork. I've heard of ham. I've heard of hotdogs. I've even heard descriptions of a particularly vile compound known as sausage. But could you tell the committee what precisely *is* scrapple?"

"Well, as you know, pork is the term for pig flesh in general. Ham is the most preferable type of pork, for those who might have developed an unfortunate taste for such things. Hotdogs are made out of the parts of the pig that don't make the grade as ham. Sausage is made out of the parts that don't qualify for hot dogs. Scrapple, then, is those parts of the pig that don't make it into sausage."

"Mister Prosecutor, what parts are those?"

The Eminent Domain wasn't ready for the answer. They got it anyway.

People were outraged. They were disgusted. Their representatives at the Archsenate initiated legal proceedings that would, if followed through to their conclusion, have involved jettisoning Justin Jeopardy into space. And it looked like they just might have the votes.

The Archsenate was deadlocked. The president's fate rested in the hands of the deciding vote, Archsenator Ringo Pippin. A deal was made: Pippin would vote for acquittal if Jeopardy would not seek another term and, instead, put all the weight and heft of his political organization behind Pippin's candidacy for president.

The acquittal was followed by a galacticam broadcast

of Jeopardy's farewell speech: "My fellow Domestic citizens, I come before you with a heavy heart. What should have been a private matter between a man and his colon erupted into a public display."

It got worse from there.

But as bad as it was for Jeopardy, it was far worse for Pippin, who decided that the moral outcry made the outgoing president's endorsement the kiss of death. After all the backroom machinations, Pippin kept Jeopardy sidelined.

Citizens of the Great Planet of ExxonMobilSunocoUnocalWorld loved three things. First was football. Second was football halftime shows: cheerleaders, marching bands and public executions. It was between the fourth and climactic fifth execution – both burnings – that the other thing ExxonMobilSunocoUnocalans loved – their dear Satrap Sajak Pickfour – announced his candidacy for 'the presidentiary.' He then sat back, watched the climactic fifth execution, then the anticlimactic sixth and seventh.

Billions of Domestic citizens voted in that election. Sajak Pickfour ended up beating Ringo Pippin by one vote. Justin Jeopardy's.

Pickfour's first executive order was, without fanfare, to rescind the ban on solid food. The middle classes were slow to pick up on this, but the Pickfour clan was quick to recapture an ancient tradition known as a *cookout* or a *barbecue,* depending on with which offshoot of the family one conversed. Newly inaugurated President Sajak Pickfour proved very fond of a side course known as baked beans. He had an inexhaustible appetite for the dish and, thus, for toilet paper.

ROMEO ROMEO

"Sanchez," General Camille Dishinstaller called into her field phone from the hallway outside President Emelem Cox-Arquette's office, "I need you to disrupt fleet-to-surface provisions ... Yes, Operation Romeo Romeo ... How soon? ... Outstanding ... How long can you keep that up? ... Outstanding."

"Hello, Carl's Jr.? ... Yes, I'd like to place an order for delivery," Cox-Arquette spoke into his own phone. "What, you don't deliver? ... You don't even take orders over the phone? ... Listen, *bubbe*, you'll take this one and you'll deliver ... 'Why?' I'll give you 'why.' First, I'm the president. Second, I'm right around the corner. Third, I'd like a hundred thousand bacon cheeseburgers, a hundred-fifty thousand chili-cheese burgers, two hundred thousand double Western bacon cheeseburgers and half a million double sourdough bacon cheeseburgers. Do the CrissCut fries come with that? ... Good ... Pop? ... Well, what has the most sugar? ... Yes, mega-size that, and I'll be calling you in about twelve hours about breakfast burritos. So what's that come to so far? ... Okey-dokey, can I put that on a credit card? ... Yes, it's a Diners Club, number five-seven-three-two ... What? You don't take Diners Club?"

☆☆☆

Around seven o'clock that night, as the second-shift manager of the Hollywood Carl's jr. took Emelem Cox-Arquette's Diners Club number, Lieutenant Colonel Sanjay Sanchez was already swinging into action.

"Branchmanager!" he called to the baby-faced lieutenant in a plaid shirt and denim overalls sitting at the communications console at the Palm Springs headquarters. "Do you remember how to FTP?"

"Yes, Sir!" the young man piped up, with fervor. "I even know how to hardcode from the command line! Did you know that ...?"

"All very well, Lieutenant, but all I need is an FTP for the moment. I want you to search Server Green-Black-Green for a folder named 'Romeo Romeo'."

"Yes Sir. Would you like to see my diagrams for a resilient optical cable network between here and Hollywood? It would feature dark-fiber redundancy and a diversity of ..."

"There'll be another battle son," the colonel said in a calming voice. "'Romeo Romeo'?"

☆☆☆

Operation Romeo Romeo had to be executed within three hours, but it didn't go according to schedule. It came in way ahead of schedule.

At 2300 Las Vegas time, the shuttle from the Domestic fleet was scheduled to arrive at Spaceport Politeness, as Friends Helping Friends had renamed Watts Barber Airbase, as Watts Barber had renamed McCarran International Airport. The shuttle contained the manna and distilled water that was to sustain the Domestic troops for the week.

Lieutenant Colonel Sanjay Sanchez's handpicked elite squad could be relied upon to deliver the goods. The key to the whole operation was the diversion and, if there was one thing that Las Vegas oozed, it was diversions.

With Lieutenant Gates Branchmanager's expertise, the files were downloaded in no time at all and distributed to the operatives in Las Vegas. Those operatives would copy the media files onto the players they had stashed in town.

Sanchez made a hardwired phone call from Palm Springs to the Vegas operatives, and the conversation was exactly one syllable long: 'Go.' Ten minutes later, a dozen twenty-foot diagonal, letterbox-dimensioned, high-definition plasma screens were being loaded out of a seemingly deserted warehouse off Blue Diamond Road onto as many flatbeds lined up on the railhead.

Within the hour, a small diesel engine backed up into the train of flatbeds, steamed forward with a series of lurches as the couplings bucked, then swung onto the main Union Pacific rail line toward the spaceport.

It pulled into the spaceport's spur and forward to the end of the line, just as the dust began to swirl on an otherwise imperceptible downdraft. The Domestic shuttle, in silence, broke through the high wispy clouds.

"Hey, Bertie. Hey, Gene," the Domestic supply sergeant said to the American engineer and fireman on the train as it came to a stop. "You're early. The craft hasn't landed yet."

They were the regular local contractors who had made the run dozens of times since the occupation began. The sergeant had no reason to believe that, many years earlier, these now scruffy, paunchy, middle-aged men were battle-hardened veterans of the Floridian and Canadian wars. For sure, he didn't know that these men, who were waiting for the day when they could return to the spaceport driving a tank rather than a locomotive, recited a loyalty oath to President Watts Barber every morning. And he had no clue that, less than two hours earlier, they had been on the receiving end of a call from Lieutenant Colonel Sanjay Sanchez.

"We can wait, Sarge," said the conductor, Bertie, with the high forehead and bushy match of eyebrows and moustache. "Gives us a chance to unload some cargo first."

"Yeah," the sergeant said. "I kinda noticed. Whatcha got back there?"

"You never seen these?" asked Gene, a tousled-haired, moon-faced man. His nonchalance managed not to seem too rehearsed. "Oh, you can't say you've seen America 'til you've seen this stuff."

"We don't have to offload right away, do we now, Gene?" Bertie asked.

"Why, no. We sure don't," Gene replied, then turned his focus back to the Domestic non-com. "Tell you what. It's gonna be a good fifteen minutes before that bird lands. Gives us plenty of time to get the sound and picture hooked up. We'll give you and your friends on board a show when they get down."

"That's very nice of you fellows," the sergeant said.

"Ain't nothing," Bertie said with a shrug.

As Bertie and Gene took off some tarps, strung some cables and tested the signals, the shuttle landed and the paperwork - so-called even though it was forced by necessity to be performed using clunky handheld electronics - was passed off and passed back.

"You folks ready?" Gene called out to the Domestic crews on the craft and around the spaceport.

The Nevada night was pierced by light - white light - and black and gray shadows.

The screen on the flatbed behind the engine glowed with the oversized, sharp-cornered W and B of the Warner Brothers logo, which were soon supplanted by the bold words, *Knute Rockne All-American.*

The screen on the following flatbed came alive with *The Santa Fe Trail.* Behind that, *Hellcats of the Navy* and then *Cattle Queen of Montana.* And so on, until the last flatbed displayed *Dark Victory.*

Gene used his disposable mobile phone to call the colonel back and report success.

Lieutenant Colonel Sanjay Sanchez allowed himself a satisfied smirk as he informed his staff.

"So that's what 'Romeo Romeo' meant," a beaming Lieutenant Branchmanager said. "R-R."

"As in 'Ronald Reagan'," the colonel summed up.

The film festival was in full swing at the spaceport. The few Americans present basked in the presence of the beloved legend whom they considered to be the founder of their country.

As they all learned in school, prior to 1980, America was ruled by a series of weak, ineffectual presidents. Middle-school social studies teachers referred to this two-hundred-year interregnum as The Age of Weenies.

It was the sainted Ronald Reagan who demonstrated that it didn't take cultivation, learning or a broad world view to rule America. All a president needed was cunning, guile, a will to power and the ability to demonstrate – whether or not it was actually true – that he was completely out of his mind.

The Americans knew every line of the film festival by heart, and shouted them out.

"Where's the rest of me?" the chorus would call out.

"Win just one for the Gipper."

"Bonzo!"

☆☆☆

Gene and Bertie helped themselves to a couple of burgers as they lazed in the engine's compartment, their end of the mission completed.

"Beam me up," Gene said.

Bertie dutifully poured him a shot of Jim Beam.

"Hey, this is really working out," Gene continued. "Ol' Dishy really knows her stuff."

"I hear this one came from Cox-Arquette," Bertie replied and took a swig himself.

"Hey, Bertie," Gene said after setting awhile in silence, "What kinda name is 'Cox-Arquette'?"

"I thought everyone knew this," Bertie said. "In the late twentieth century, a TV star named Courtney Cox married a movie star named David Arquette."

"Oh," Gene said, then sat in silence again for a moment's meditation. "Good thing she didn't marry Chris Tucker."

That hadn't occurred to Bertie, who took another shot of Beam and added, "Or Bob Uecker."

☆☆☆

It was all new to the Domestic troops. As they walked along in the course of their duties – or just to look busy – their ears would hear a picket-fence pattern of cinematic dialogue, lovingly preserved by a grateful nation and delivered via highest quality sound reinforcement gear arrayed by expert technicians. One by one, the soldiers of the Eminent Domain wandered past a compelling scene, turned and were mesmerized. They sat on the ground or pulled over chairs, benches or crates. In rapt, respectful awe, they watched the master at work, bringing black-and-white simplicity to a universe of pervasive digital media.

Sitting and staring at the screens under the starry but

moonless night sky, the Domestic troops began to sense that something was missing from the movie experience. The lucky few seated in the back, who found willing copulation partners, were - during a three-minute distraction - spared this sense of longing. Nevertheless, soon it affected everyone. As they sprawled out, eyes fixated, they each felt a fidgeting in their hands and an emptiness in their mouths.

That's when the second train pulled up.

In the first train, though, Bertie and Gene barely noticed the vibrations on the track, a fifth of bourbon acting as a finely-tuned suspension.

"To Ronnie!" Bertie proposed.

"To Ronnie!" Gene agreed, and they tipped their shot glasses back.

Bertie quickly refilled them.

"He won the Cold War!" Gene proclaimed. They both drank again and slopped a refill into their glasses.

"He was great in 'Cavalry Charge'!" Bertie replied, as they drank once more and spilled whisky into their glasses, but more on the floor.

"He was the model for future American statesmen from Bush to Schwartzengrogger ... Bush to Schwingernocker ... Bush to Bush!" Gene offered. They drank. They tried and failed to refill.

"He nailed Bette Davis, Olivia de Havilland *and* Doris Day!" Bertie announced, and they took turns swigging, in greed and need, from the bottle.

The half dozen crew members on that other train were completely sober.

They were America's most skilled assassins, Lieutenant Colonel Sanjay Sanchez's personally-trained elite squad, under the tactical control of Gunnery Sergeant Chuck-Claude Spamblocker. Silently, stealthily, surreptitiously, hooded figures jumped off the flatbeds even before the train had come to a complete stop.

These shock troops were trained in every form of combat practiced on Earth. They were qualified in every type of weapon on Earth, from the largest artillery battery to the most basic improvised cudgels. With bare hands, the least experienced of them could kill an enemy combatant thirty different ways.

That night, they threaded unobtrusively through the crowd handing out bacon cheeseburgers, CrissCut fries and forty-four-ounce orange sodas.

One of them pulled out a lighter and a pack of Marlboros, but Gunny Spamblocker smacked them out of her hand.

"You want a war crime on your conscience?" he scolded.

☆☆☆

Coder, LT3IL8IL1, was among those watching *Angels Wash Their Faces,* in which the youthful future president played a crusading district attorney out to clear the name of the Bowery Boys.

Absentmindedly, unaware that the double-bacon cheeseburger was even in his right hand, Coder's elbow levitated to his mouth. He took a bite.

Raised on tasteless, textureless food substitutes, he was so overwhelmed by the fluffiness of the bun, the crispness of the bacon and the sweet dripping of the cheese that he could no longer focus on the movie's intricate plot, rapier wit and grand performances. The smoky patty in the center was a taste of primal carnage that he could never have imagined. In every bite of the sandwich, there was also a pulpy, crackly aftertaste that, although unpleasant, he considered part of the irresistible experience.

Coder wolfed down the sandwich in seven mouthfuls. Before the last one was completely swallowed, he took a long swig of citrus that must have come from the primordial Garden itself. Saltiness, in the form of the fries, then made its debut on the infantry clone's taste buds.

As Ronald Reagan dramatically made his case, with young Gabe's life in the balance, Coder found himself out of burger, out of fries, with twenty-two ounces of carbonated orange nectar cupped, lonely, in his left hand ... and he craved more. As if he had willed it into existence, another sandwich was in his grip. It had the same fluffy bun, crispy bacon, drippy cheese and smoky meat, but he was pleased that it lacked the pulpy crackle of the first round.

Unknown to Coder, Gunny Spamblocker had spread the word to his comrades:

"Lose the wrappers," he'd whispered into his handset, his voice instantly received in five earpieces. "These guys are dumber than we thought."

☆☆☆

Not a single Friends Helping Friends soldier's life was lost that night but, in a less literal sense, they all were.

The siren call of Carl's jr. would not be denied. There were fewer than a hundred Domestic troopers at the spaceport that night, but all those stationed on the ground shared sleeping quarters. Soon the bare floors of their barracks ran red with ketchup. The manna taken off the shuttle was left rotting in the next day's desert sun, while the craft itself returned to the mothership laden with cholesterol, trans fat and indigestible glucose – mega-sized.

Overnight, the Carl's jr. chain had the better part of

three million new customers and struggled to keep up with demand. With the fervor of the religiously converted – or perhaps of the newly addicted – Domestic troops gobbled the nutritionally-challenged fare almost as fast as America could make it, which was pretty fast.

In short order, diseases that had never affected Domestic citizens were now endemic among the expeditionary force. The doctors who had, with such expertise, preserved life in the face of battlefield butchery struggled in vain against diabetes, hypertension, embolisms, aneurisms, strokes, heart attacks. There was nothing to stop them.

☆☆☆

"OK, great job, everyone," concluded General Camille Dishinstaller, addressing her entire senior staff assembled in what was once the teachers' lounge of an elementary school in Palm Springs. Following her lead, the attendees were all in battledress uniform again. "Dismissed."

The assemblage stood up and headed for the door. As the staff meeting broke up, the general added, "Stick around, Sanjay."

Lieutenant Colonel Sanjay Sanchez stayed behind.

"Ma'am?"

"Remember some months ago when I told you to forward all intel to Hollywood?"

"Yes, Ma'am."

"It would've been nice if you'd forwarded the codes as well."

Sanchez, a battle-hardened veteran, whose most impressive decorations lined his face and could never be taken away, refused to react to the rebuke.

After a silence, the general continued.

"I have to be able to count on you, Sanchez. There's too much at stake for foul-ups like this."

"Ma'am," Sanchez began, carefully. "With all due

respect, when you picked me from a hundred applicants for this post, you knew I was a war fighter and weak on the administrative end."

"Thanks to the delay in interpreting Celltower's reports, there's been a hell of a lot more war to fight," the general replied. "Anyway, we are where we are. Don't screw up like that again. Are we clear?"

☆☆☆

Gene and Bertie were back in their warehouse off Blue Diamond Road.

The tide of the battle had, without question, turned in the favor of America's Well Regulated Militia. They were no longer keeping up the ruse of running the train shuttling manna from the spaceport to the Strip. Only prisoners still ate manna.

Now, grinning with an optimism Americans had almost forgotten, they were using their 50,000 square foot cinderblock shell to assemble tanks from components they had been amassing and storing for months.

They took a break from the work, which challenged both body and mind.

Water would do that day.

"If you'd have asked me just a few weeks ago, I wouldn't have said so," Bertie said, slumped against a half-track, water bottle in hand, "but I think we're actually gonna win."

"I never had any doubt," Gene replied, sanding away at a last, stubborn patch of rust on the unarmored skeleton of a tank in the making. Done, he stretched, walked over to Bertie and sat down beside him. "Those burgers are really doing the trick."

They tapped polyethylene water bottles together with an unsatisfactory, dull *thwunk*!

"It's hard to imagine all the nasty stuff inside them, for

which we've developed a tolerance," Bertie said.

"I don't even want to think about it," Gene replied. "Not just the grease and gristle - but salmonella, botulism, E. coli. Uggh!"

"But we've seen it ourselves," Bertie said and waxed mystical. "Scattered about, in their overturned war machines - *dead!* - slain by the putrefactive and disease bacteria against which their systems were unprepared."

"Bertie ..." Gene started, his eyes rolling. *No, don't get started.*

"Slain, after all our devices had failed, by the humblest things that ..."

"Bertie ..."

"By the toll of a billion deaths, we have bought our birthright of the earth, and it is ours against all ..."

"Bertie ..."

"The destruction of Sennacherib has been repeated, the Angel of Death had slain them in the ..."

"Bertie," Gene hollered, out of patience. "Shut up!"

☆☆☆

But the human form, especially after centuries away from its natural environment, was nothing if not adaptable.

Some were lost, but not as many as America's Acting President Emelem Cox-Arquette or General Camille Dishinstaller had planned.

Coder, LT3IL8IL1, for instance, neither went into shock from diabetes nor burst a plaque-constricted artery. He did, however, become the first individual in the history of the Eminent Domain to develop the condition known in America as 'pizza face.' Shortly thereafter, he became the first individual in the history of the Eminent Domain to die of embarrassment.

Even after that tragedy - and that of his clone, who tried cleaning his weapon with fryer grease on his fingers, plus that of his other clone, who in error surmised that when an anthropomorphic piece of plastic is marked "CHOKING HAZARD" that meant he should be sure to chew it thoroughly – the Domestic military continued to dig in.

There was still a war on.

WHAT HAPPENS IN VEGAS

The council is formed," the old woman said. Ronald Reagan's face, carved on Mount Rushmore, hovered over her shoulder. The younger members of the circle saw her almost in silhouette, her features obscured by the glare and smoke of the crackling campfire. The flicker of flame revealed a woman wearing the buckskins of a Sioux elder, whose dust-blown skin was many shades darker than one might expect from a member of that culture.

Respect was given her, though none was commanded. To hear her quiet wisdom, it seemed as if the rustling wind and the howling coyote both gave pause.

"As Peace Chief," she continued, "it is my honor to convene this coming together. In this sad time, it is also my solemn duty to pass the talking stick to the War Chief. You know him as a man of many brave acts: Shoots at the Stars."

"Thank you for your kind words, Fire from the Lake," said the man to her right, maybe ten years younger. "We all await the day when you shall again lead us in time of peace. But we must deal first with the invaders."

If Shoots at the Stars had anything else to say on the subject, it was cut off by an outburst from a young, fiery-eyed brave who demanded to be heard, even though he did not hold the talking stick.

"We must never give them a moment's rest," he began. "We must bring the battle to these star soldiers in their barracks and in their travels. We must slaughter them all! Leave their bodies hanging from high places as a warning to their leaders! Relentlessly attack until the last stragglers run back to the safety of their own worlds! Only then will we have rescued our beloved Earth Mother from those who would destroy her!"

He paused to draw a breath, and Shoots at the Stars took the opportunity to steer the discussion back on track.

"Your words hold great courage, Should Switch to Decaf," the War Chief said. "But we can only use the resources we have. Who can give us a battle plan that will turn away the star soldiers?"

In earnest, one young man said, "Perhaps there is still a peaceful solution. They wanted revenge. They have taken revenge. How many of the Mother's daughters and sons have been lost to the sky soldiers? They have their retribution. Surely we can negotiate a truce?"

Fire from the Lake herself spoke in response.

"You are a gentle spirit and a wise one, Stuffed in a Gym Locker," she said. "But we know no neutral party who would host such talks. If there were, the star soldiers would not heed the ruling. It is a sadness to me that this is the season for war. And we must answer Shoots at the Stars' question: How do we turn away these invaders?"

"We do not have sufficient force to take the battle to them," Shoots at the Stars continued. "We must use stealth and cunning."

"I volunteer to lead a scouting party into their city and find a weakness," Should Switch to Decaf said, rising to his feet.

"Go with the Mother's blessings," Shoots at the Stars said and then added, just to be on the safe side, "Take Stuffed in a Gym Locker with you."

M. Griffin Croupier VII had been on the verge of tears since mid-morning. That is, since the mail from back home arrived.

He'd held it together for hours and hours. Going to meetings, chairing meetings, reading memos, writing memos, shredding memos; the day would have been a pointless grind even without the devastating news.

After-hours socializing with the top military officers was no more pleasant. Sanmateo Veecey brought down his turntable from his office and inflicted his musical tastes on the rest of the command-and-control team. Having had enough, Croupier excused himself from the sectioned-off ballroom early, his retinue of bodyguards swarming annoyingly.

A moment later, he was too wrapped up in his own problems to notice the music had stopped.

"Griff!" General Veecey called out after Croupier, following him into the Bellagio's opulent lobby, frayed ponytail swinging behind him, voice scratchy from lack of sleep, his own newly puffy security detail in front and behind. "Wait up a second."

"Hi, Mat," Croupier said as he pressed for the elevator.

"You look down," Veecey pried. His suspicions that Croupier was interested in Appdev still occupied the corner of his mind that wasn't focused on the musical cache. "Anything I need to know about?"

"Got some bad news from back home. I'll deal with it."

"If you say so," Veecey said, rubbing the bags under his eyes. "I just thought you might need to talk."

"All I have to say is, love is hard."

"Tell me about it," Veecey said, then decided that maybe Croupier could be coaxed into an exchange of information. "I've been in an unrequited non-relationship for longer than I care to admit. At least you're married."

And before he even said the last word, he understood.

"Oh, Griff, I didn't realize. That's awful."

Veecey, sensing his friend's heartache and realizing that Croupier had, in truth, never been his romantic rival, went to put an arm on his shoulder. Croupier stepped back instinctively, not wishing to be touched in any way.

"This is the life I chose," Croupier said, after regaining his composure. "He chose something else."

"Look, if there's anything...."

"Thanks, Mat. You're a good friend. But I have to sort this out myself."

Then the elevator came and took Croupier away.

Veecey turned to one of his guards, now grown obese, and still wheezing from the long walk.

"Did he say, 'he'?"

Without another word, Veecey went up to his room and lay down for a long-overdue six-hour nap.

☆☆☆

Croupier got off on the top floor and ran into that adorable room service boy – the one with the nice butt.

"Good afternoon, Sir," he said with a deferential, but decidedly heterosexual, air.

"It's afternoon at any rate," Croupier replied.

"Anything the Bellagio can do for you, Sir?" he said with an arched eyebrow.

"Not unless you've got a machine in this room that'll take away all my troubles," Croupier said, his head bowed to hide the mist in his eyes.

"Well then, Sir, we're in luck."

☆☆☆

The chili-cheese burgers were a life-changing experience. An hour later, that is, after she got off the toilet.

Never having had solid food before, Iman Appdev hadn't

ever had a bowel movement. That, too, was a sensual treat for which she was unprepared. In recent years, the Eminent Domain's rich and powerful had become more open about their once-clandestine habit of eating. Lifestyle shows on the galacticam were chock-full of trendy features on soft seats, oversized bowls, brilliant-colored tanks, adjustable water flow, jet-powered suction and soft-as-babies-kisses toilet paper. Toilet paper! She never dreamed she'd ever need it!

She stood up from the bowl, let her trousers drop to the floor, stepped out of her unlaced boots, turned around and flushed. She watched her specimen swirl helplessly down the porcelain as she luxuriated in the downdraft. Appdev washed her hands thoroughly before opening the door but declined to waste time with perfumes, dressing gowns, negligees, hair ribbons or any other touches of glamor. Instead, she all but pushed the bathroom door off the hinges and presented herself naked to the American she knew as Porsche.

"I am yours," she said, her pupils so wide G.Q. Celltower thought he was staring into two small pockets of midnight, even though the late summer sun still dominated the sky. "You may do with me as you will."

So he told her, in precise but not clinical terms, exactly what he will.

Her jaw gaped and eyebrows arched. She continued to stand there in unadorned flesh, letting him admire her, suddenly very shy.

"That's not what I meant."

"Is there some taboo against that where you come from?"

"Oh, no, not at all," she said. "But the purpose is strictly for procreation to repopulate the Eminent Domain's worlds."

"And for no other purpose?" he asked coolly.

"Well, in the case of homosexuals, to foster intimacy upon which to build a lifetime commitment, with an obligation to adopt children and raise them to be good

Domestic citizens," she explained. "I thought you might want to cuddle or hold hands or play a board game."

"We have different ways on Earth," Celltower said and, sensing that was the end of her half-hearted argument, began showering his conquest with kisses from the nape of her neck to the soles of her feet.

"I suppose I am a guest here," she continued, feeling the need to rationalize. "And we're supposed to be – stop that! – to be sensitive to our cultural differences ... Hey, that tickles! ... And perhaps in your ... *Holy Hanna*!"

At that point, words failed her.

As Celltower dipped her gently onto the canopied bed, removed his own clothes and pressed himself down on her, her last coherent sentence was, "I can't believe I'm doing this without a license!"

☆☆☆

"My turn!" Stuffed in a Gym Locker shouted for the third time, as his compatriot gave up the seat in front of the telescope.

"Fine," Should Switch to Decaf replied, as he poured himself another cup from his thermos.

They were holed up in the attic of an abandoned house on a hill, overlooking the Strip. From that vantage point, they had a commanding view over most of the Friends Helping Friends command-and-control structure.

That included Iman Appdev's window.

Peering through the scope, Stuffed in a Gym Locker could see that she and her unidentified partner were absently munching on a bag of French fries. Silk sheets hid anything worth seeing.

"I missed the whole thi-i-i-i-ng," he whined.

"Tell you what, Gym," Should Switch to Decaf offered, "if they do it again, you get to watch."

"You think they'll do it again, Deke?"

"I bet you fifty pounds of buffalo they're having sex again by the time the first star comes out."

The Terrahist, known to his friend as Gym, did satisfy his prurient interest that evening but the man he called Deke reneged on the bet, saying that what Gym witnessed wasn't really sex, citing the long-established Clinton Distinction.

The unidentified man, for whom the Terrahist pair developed an abiding respect, left immediately afterward.

The Domestic officer lay down in bed, tried to keep still but, through the telescope, the men from the Great Plains could see she couldn't get comfortable.

☆☆☆

The design of the bedspread was ornate and ugly enough to mask the evidence of Iman Appdev's ruptured hymen. The French doors to the balcony were flung open to the desert night, the wind carrying away the bouquet of sex.

There was a knock at the door.

Thinking it was her man coming back for more, Appdev didn't bother to throw on a robe when she answered it. Her afterglow evaporated.

"Griff?"

"Can I come in?" an addled M. Griffin Croupier VII slurred.

She couldn't say no to such a dear man in such an awful condition. But she did then throw on the robe before noting that Croupier didn't seem aroused by her nakedness, as had her American lover.

She sat Croupier down on the sofa and asked what was wrong.

"It's these beverages they keep in the room."

"What beverages? Where?" she asked, sitting down alongside him.

"In there - that thing - the cabinet under the window," he said, gesturing with his wrist.

"Oh, there are drinks in there?" Appdev asked. "I never looked. I thought that's where they kept the spare linen."

"It's called a mini-bar. One of the staff told me about it."

"What's in there?"

"Really institious ... um ... insidient ... um, confusing stuff. It looks like water, tastes like fire and plays havoc with your judgment."

"Judgment has been in short supply tonight."

"Yeah, no kidding," he said, lacking interest. Then he boomed, "This is about *me!*"

"Sorry."

"Yeah, everybody's sorry. You're sorry. I'm sorry I spent my career trying to make morons like Sajak Pickfour look like they can tie their own shoes! Mat Veecey's sorry because he's in an unrequisited ... uh ... unrequired ... uh ... he loves a girl who doesn't know it. My husband's sorry because now he has to be my ex-husband. And we're all stuck on this sorry excuse for a planet, on this sorry excuse for a mission!"

Having no response, she just mouthed 'sorry' one more time.

"S'awright," Croupier choked out, right before the uncontrollable sobbing commenced.

Appdev went to get a box of tissues.

"He left me! Just like that! After all these years! 'I can't take coming in second to your career all the time.' That's what he ... Steve ... that's what Steve said."

"Oh, you poor thing," she said, putting an arm around him.

"Don't want your pity," he snarled and pulled away.

"What do you want?"

"Another drink."

"Is that wise?"

"Is anything about this occupation wise?"

"Good point," she said and went over to the mini-bar. "Let's see what they've got. Merlott? Sounds dreadful.

Drambwhy, Drambwhee ... How do you pronounce that? Oh, here we go! This sounds nice and calming."

And so Iman Appdev and Griff Croupier introduced each other to Southern Comfort.

And, before they passed out, they discovered just how impaired their judgment could become.

An hour later, Croupier became conscious enough to realize that there was such a thing as enough toxins in his system to confuse his sex drive. Disgusted by what just happened, he grabbed his clothes and snuck out.

"I cannot believe that," Gym said, watching Croupier close the door with great care behind him.

"Yes, two men in one night," Deke replied.

"And that second one, unless I am mistaken, is their Peace Chief."

"I believe you are probably correct, Gym," Deke said. "But I'm sure that, even if he is not Croupier, he is light in the moccasins."

"She must be a remarkable woman."

"Wait," Deke said eagerly. She's waking up."

Through the dimness of waking, Iman Appdev heard a repeated, bold knock on the door. It was a surprise that Griff Croupier wasn't there next to her. Maybe it was him. Maybe it was her insatiable American. But who knew? She took the precaution of putting her robe on this time.

"General!"

"'General' is taking the night off," Sanmateo Veecey said, refreshed and clear-eyed. "Just call me 'Mat'."

"Well, come in ... Mat."

He did. And she offered him a seat.

"No thanks, he replied, I won't be staying long. I just came to tell you something. I love you. I have since I first saw you. You were in a review formation with two dozen other Academy graduates freshly assigned to my command. But I couldn't take my eyes off you for a second."

"I don't know what to ..."

He cut her off. It was apparent he had rehearsed this and, contrary to what he said a minute before, he would be staying long.

"I can't live without you any longer. I'll do anything you ask. I'll resign my commission. I'll even give up music. Just stay with me," he said. "Please."

She stood there for a moment, replaying the events of that evening: the bodily pleasures that had been denied her, the surrender to lust, the improbable encounter with a man whom she admired and had befriended and now, this profession of undying love.

The robe came off.

☆☆☆

"No way," Gym said.

"Yes," affirmed Deke, whose turn it was at the telescope. "I recognize this man. She is with Veecey, the star soldiers' War Chief. She must be of great importance, for a warrior to be so willing to be her third partner of the night."

"You think he knows that?"

"These people have very strange ways," Should Switch to Decaf began. "But even if he is unaware, we still know that this woman holds Veecey's heart and has also captivated Croupier. She is the key. We cannot capture either of those men, for they are too well-guarded. We can, however, bring her back to the Council with us. With her as hostage, we can force the leaders of these invaders to leave us in peace, never to return. We can triumph over this enemy and prove to all humanity why Mother Earth must forever reign supreme over all her daughters and sons, no matter how far they roam!"

"Have you ever tried yoga?"

Should Switch to Decaf's only response was a momentary full-face twitch followed by a terse "Let's go."

"Never?"

"No, Iman, not before tonight."

And so Iman Appdev engaged, for the first time, in pillow talk.

"Really? I mean, you're a good-looking guy. A high-ranking officer. A musician."

"And rich," Sanmateo Veecey interjected.

"That too. And this was your first time? At your age?"

"You're making it sound pathetic."

"It kinda is."

"Guess I was just waiting for the right woman."

"In that case, it's not pathetic," she allowed. "It's sweet."

"And how about you?" he asked.

"What about me?"

"Was this your first time?"

She propped herself up on an elbow and stared into his eyes. She considered what a devout Candorian, who subscribed to a code of absolute honesty, could say in this situation.

"Mat, I can in all honesty tell you, I have never had sex before this night."

She had seen him proud before, and honored, and humbled, but that was the first time she ever saw him smug.

"Well, as much as I would love to stay here, I'd better go back to my own billet. We need to keep this quiet for now."

"Yes. Oh, yes. Not a word to anyone. For right now."

He wondered why she seemed so confused.

So it was not too long after General Veecey returned to his own suite, with an armed and armored sentry at every door and window, that Captain Appdev was awoken again that night.

This time, she didn't bother putting on the robe because so far that night, it had turned out to be a wasted effort. She didn't even ask who it was.

Which is how she found herself with a face full of chloroform, on the back of a flatbed truck, heading north and east.

THE MORNING AFTER

As dawn broke over Las Vegas, General Sanmateo Veecey appeared at Iman Appdev's door, bearing a bouquet of orchids, red roses and baby's breath. After a moment, he knocked again. After a minute went by, he set the bundle, *scherzando*, on the doorstep. As he rose to stand, though, pain crashed in on his skull.

He had risen into the heavy silver tray carried by M. Griffin Croupier VII. The contents of the pot of coffee scalded both men and the tall glass of tomato juice splashed Veecey's face, while the celery stalk it contained perched on his cap.

"Uh, hi."

"Uh, hi."

"Uh, hi," came a voice a few steps down the hall. It was G.Q. Celltower. He was carrying a breakfast burrito and a long-necked bottle of ice-cold beer.

Without another monosyllable, the three men picked up an ashcan from ten paces down the hall and rammed down the door to Appdev's suite.

There was no trace of her. Veecey's and Croupier's protection detail scoured the suite for any clues. The ever-vigilant, yet utterly discreet, teams found nothing suspicious. Nothing in the least bit telling, at all, anywhere in the room, least of all on the bedsheets.

Veecey got on his comnet gear, trying to locate her. No answer, so he called the duty officer and reported Appdev missing.

Croupier got on the house phone and checked with the hotel's front desk. Nobody had seen her leave since the shift came on an hour earlier.

Celltower zeroed in on the French windows, noting the drapes were open. He stepped out on the balcony, took his Militia-issued field glasses out from under his room service livery and surveyed the buildings in direct line of sight. In a building where every other window was abuzz with morning activity, one loft was abandoned, its window wide open, one single incandescent bulb lit, swinging in the wind from a cord, a couple of mattresses thrown down at odd angles on the floor on either side of a mini fridge.

He then strode over to the bed, where none of the bodyguards noticed any strange odors. None at all. He sniffed, then ran his hand over the sheets and pillowcases.

"She was kidnapped," Celltower told Veecey and Croupier. "They used chloroform. You can still smell it; the pillow is still cold to the touch. I think there were two of them; that's how many mattresses are lying on the floor of an abandoned apartment up on that ridge," he continued, gesturing out of the French doors.

Veecey and Croupier looked at each other, then at Celltower, then back at each other, then back at Celltower, then, in unison, asked, "Who the hell are you?"

☆☆☆

Between them, Veecey and Croupier had a dozen armed and specially trained bodyguards, albeit all a little on the stout side, four of whom were standing post in Appdev's suite. It became clear that the trim, athletic G.Q. Celltower was no ordinary busboy.

In answer to 'Who the hell are you?' he replied, 'Your only shot in hell of seeing Iman Appdev alive again.' Then he said nothing else until Veecey took the hint and ordered the entire security contingent into the hall.

He gave his real name - what did it matter now? - and explained what he was doing there. And when he had been there last. And why. And how. And then how. And asked if either of them wanted to know what really drove her crazy.

The two Domestic overlords declined such information. Veecey couldn't mask that he was scandalized, dejected, crushed. Croupier, whose knack for persuasiveness had served him very well in his career, concentrated his considerable mental energy on computing moves to secure a three-way.

"Sorry? What was the question?" Croupier asked an hour later.

Apparently, Veecey and Celltower were working on some sort of rescue plan. Of course. That was the first move. That must be what he said 'Yes of course' to some time earlier.

"We're ordering up breakfast," Veecey said. "Do you want anything?"

Declining toast, poached eggs, even corned beef itself, Croupier ordered coffee and juice.

One forty-five-second phone call later, and they were back to business.

"The General was just asking me," Celltower said, "where I think Iman was taken."

"I know," Croupier lied. There was an awkward silence. "And what did you say?"

"I said I didn't know."

"Oh."

"But I know someone who might."

Celltower told Veecey and Croupier what he considered was the correct next move. They agreed. Now it was Celltower's turn to make a phone call.

And it wasn't to room service.

Intending to return to her command center in Palm Springs, Camille Dishinstaller left the provisional government's Hollywood office for the last time. Sanjay Sanchez was capably holding down the fort, but there was only so much Hollywood she could take.

She waited a moment outside the former motion picture theater for her SUV and driver. She had grown fond of her driver who, in addition to serving as a bodyguard, also served as a companion - someone to talk with to pass the time on long drives, like the one ahead. But the young woman was first her bodyguard.

But the vehicle wasn't anywhere in sight. That's when it registered with Dishinstaller that something was wrong.

One shot rang out from a third-floor fire escape across the street. It lodged in the masonry of the building's façade, not six inches behind her and just a hair to her right. A lead bullet - that could only mean her own people! These were Sanchez's shock troops!

Dishinstaller had time to register the betrayal but not react to it as the next shot rang out. It lodged in a planter that once contained a rubber tree, but now contained only dirt, if one didn't count the bullet. A third bullet came from down the sidewalk and passed not an inch in front of the general, shattering the sunglasses that had been hanging around her neck.

Before the echoes of the three rifle reports died down, the muffled sound of rubber-soled athletic shoes came rushing in from the direction of the last shot.

In a second, civilian-clad but manifestly expert troops had her surrounded on three sides: left, front and right. They were, in order, standing, crouching and lying flat. Their small arms were trained on, in order, her head, chest and belly. A fourth member of this elite squad came in unseen from behind, leg-tackling Dishinstaller.

She landed on her buttocks and an athletic shoe kicked her shoulders roughly to the ground. A perfectly placed fist lodged in Dishinstaller's solar plexus, leaving her gasping for air. She stared up with astonished eyes to see four pistols zeroed in on her heart and, only a pace back, three rifles pointing into her right eye.

Above them all, Dishinstaller recognized the face of the most dangerous enlisted man Sanjay Sanchez ever trained.

"We just want to talk," Gunnery Sergeant Chuck-Claude Spamblocker said.

It wasn't much of a conversation. These were tough, battle-hardened veterans who knew all there was to know about small-unit tactics. But they didn't seem very inquisitive about strategy. In fact, they didn't ask her about a thing. Not that she could answer, being gagged as well as bound and blindfolded and all.

The gag, cuffs and blindfold came off after only a couple of hours. As she suspected, it was her adjutant, Colonel Sanjay Sanchez himself, loosening her bonds. She was sitting on a chair and Sanchez sat next to her. The chairs were of the kind that were plush, overstuffed, accommodating of girth, yet could be stacked in a corner. The shock troops stood by silently, unobtrusively, yet ominously.

"You!" she accused the battle-scarred face in front of her. "Why didn't I see this coming?"

"Beg your pardon, Ma'am," the colonel replied, "but this isn't what it looks like."

She knew where she was: The Bellagio. The current seat of occupational power, erstwhile presidential palace: eternal casino. Judging by the opulent décor of long-ago times and faraway lands, she was in one of the rooms named after one of the legends of the martial arts.

"This is the Michelangelo Room."

"No, Ma'am. This is the Donatello. Michelangelo is down the hall."

"So why am I here?" the general asked. "If this was a power grab, I'd be dead by now."

"We have a plan to get rid of the space monkeys once and for all," Sanchez said, "but we need your go-ahead."

"Must be quite a plan. We're right in the middle of their cozy little ..."

In walked Sanmateo Veecey, her opposite number. She knew him right away from the news pictures. The ponytail looked a little frayed and grayer than she expected.

"General Dishinstaller, I'm honored to meet you at last," he said, extending his hand in greeting.

If their positions were reversed, Dishinstaller thought, she'd have ordered him to stand at attention. But Veecey's body language had more to do with inviting her to stand up and look him squarely in the eye.

She shook his hand.

"Look," he said, "nobody wants us off this rock more than we do ourselves. But we can't do that until we get a few things settled. Let's settle them."

He peeled a chair off a nearby stack as they both sat down.

Dishinstaller resisted ordering the American fighters behind her to shoot him, and thereby lost the chance. Veecey's security detail entered the room a moment later.

For every armed American, there was an armed invader. Sanchez sat at Dishinstaller's right and Croupier sat at Veecey's.

Then Dishinstaller was dumbstruck when G.Q. Celltower came in and positioned himself as the moderator.

"Celltower!" the American commander exclaimed. "You set this up?"

"Sorry about the rough stuff, General," he said. "We can

end the occupation in a matter of days, but it means cooperating with the Domestic forces in a joint operation against the Terrahists."

"So why kidnap me?" she asked.

"We weren't sure how President Cox-Arquette would feel about it. Worst comes to worst, we figured you'd want it to look like you were here by force."

"If it's any consolation, we don't know how President Pickfour will react either," a nervous Croupier said, rubbing fingers over his moustache. "We're going on our own authority."

Dishinstaller mulled over this for a while, her face a grim, unreadable war mask. All at once, she relaxed her face into a more reflective, receptive shape.

"OK, I'm over the shock," she said. "What's the situation?"

"My adjutant has been taken prisoner by Terrahist forces," Veecey explained. "We don't know where she was taken. So I guess our first order of business is to figure out where they're based."

"Maybe I can help there," Dishinstaller offered. "I know a little bit about them. We grew up together."

"I didn't know that," Sanchez said, as every eyebrow in the room arched.

"There are Terrahist movements all over Earth. Most are people disenchanted with the planet's recent history," Dishinstaller recounted. "They gravitated toward primitive, indigenous cultures. In this hemisphere, that meant the pre-Columbian cultures. In America, that meant the Sioux of the Northern Plains."

"How do you know all this?" Veecey asked.

"I grew up in Nebraska, so I know more than a few of these folk," Dishinstaller replied. "Can't say I disagree with them about their aims but, When All Hell Broke Loose, they were completely wrongheaded."

"Glad we can agree at least on that much," Veecey said.

"Hey, three years ago I barely knew you guys existed. Why would I want to start a fight with you?" Dishinstaller asked. "Anyway, you want to find your adjutant, you can narrow your search to the area north of Oklahoma and east of the Rockies."

"That's still a lot of territory," Sanchez volunteered.

"I could narrow it down to about a dozen locations where they consider the ground sacred," Dishinstaller said. "No guarantees, but those are the most likely places."

"That would be very helpful," Veecey said. "The sensors on our orbital craft can pinpoint them from there."

For most of the occupation, the Terrahists were indeed concentrated in the traditional Sioux territories. But their range grew with their numbers and expanded along the West Coast.

The new Terrahists had access to Domestic Raysprayer weapons. Since most of them were veterans of the pre-insurgency Well Regulated Militia, they also benefited from being trained by officers who had learned their craft from the most proficient strategist on the planet: Camille Dishinstaller.

And none of them had any interest in seeing America ruled by anyone but Fire from the Lake or Shoots at the Stars.

As a splinter cell gathered in inland California, just south of the edge of the devastation that destroyed Oregon and much of its neighboring areas, they planned an initiative that Dishinstaller would have considered very clever, had she not already thought of it herself.

☆☆☆

Even with the narrowed parameters, there were still thousands of square kilometers of Midwest to comb through.

One of Sanmateo Veecey's aides, a second lieutenant

inevitably named Daytrader, had set up monitors in the Donatello Room so that Veecey, Dishinstaller and their respective comrades could see, in real time, what the reconnaissance team in orbit was seeing.

"I wouldn't have believed it," Veecey said. "There's so much land out there. And it's all flat and all brown and all the same, no matter where you go."

"Now imagine going to high school there," Dishinstaller retorted. "Hold on. What's that?"

She pointed at the monitor. The monitor was pointed at a spot between the Black Hills and the Badlands. For an area that was never heavily populated there seemed, from space, to be a lot of people and vehicles coming in and out.

"Anything new?" asked M. Griffin Croupier VII, who had stuck his head in.

"Yeah, I think we just located the bad guys," a husky female voice replied, as a technician confirmed that Iman Appdev's unique heat signature was on that grid.

Croupier was at that moment stunned by the sight of Generals Camille Dishinstaller and Sanmateo Veecey hunched over the same monitor.

"Um, OK. I guess that's good news," Croupier assessed. "I hope everyone can take some bad news."

All eyes were on the Eminent Domain's civilian emissary.

"First of all, there's been another forest fire. At least a million acres have been torched, east of Modesto."

Dishinstaller shrugged as if to say, *I had nothing to do with it.*

Veecey nodded. *I know. You never use the same tactic twice.*

They exchanged a glance. *Terrahists.*

"They used Raysprayers set on 'ignite' and I'm sorry ... but the news just keeps getting worse," Croupier said.

"I have a training camp around there with five thousand recruits at any given time," Dishinstaller realized with a start.

"How could it get worse?"

"President Pickfour is coming again."

"You have got to be kidding me," Veecey said. "Why would he come into a war zone where the situation is so unsettled, right after a catastrophe like that?"

"To show that everything is going according to plan."

"That doesn't make any sense," piped in Lieutenant Colonel Sanjay Sanchez, as he dialed Palm Springs to see if the Militia staff there had any news on the training camp east of Modesto. He was soon to hear more very bad news.

"It doesn't have to make sense," Croupier countered. "It's an election year."

TERRAHISTS

Captain Iman Appdev woke up, her head resting on green grass and brown dirt, her wrists and ankles bound with twine.

From the grogginess she felt, she knew she had been drugged.

From the sounds in the distance and the smell and taste of the air, she knew she was in a place of rivers and grain and chirping birds; how far away from the desert dust of Las Vegas she had no way of telling.

From the bruises on her bare arms and breasts, she knew she'd been knocked around some on her journey to wherever she now found herself.

From the numbness in her hands and feet, she knew she had lost circulation.

From the soreness between her legs, she knew she'd had one hell of a night.

A fact little known among people who have never been knocked out is that, upon waking, one tends to focus on something positive. The faces of her three paramours flickered past her mind's eye rapidly, repeatedly, randomly, like a deck of cards being shuffled.

Her lips involuntarily puckered, but only for a second. She was OK, she realized, just a little banged up from being shipped, unconscious and naked, for what had to be hundreds of miles.

She knew she had to deal with the emotional fallout of losing her maidenhead, seducing a homosexual and taking a man's virginity all on the same night. She also decided that could take years, so best not to start at that moment.

The petroleum smell of ground vehicles wafted past her nostrils, accompanied by the roar of internal combustion. So she was sure she was still on Earth and, she was guessing, she was still somewhere in America.

Appdev glanced around the room she found herself in. It wasn't a room precisely. It was tall, conical and made from a material she first assumed was some sort of synthetic canvas. Staring hard enough at it, she could see the pores where the fur of some poor beast had been plucked. A wave of revulsion shook her. She sat up with a jolt.

That's when she noticed the guard who was stationed inside the tent with her. After years in military service to the Eminent Domain, she was inured to men seeing her naked, yet she was grateful for the small kindness of having a female sentry keeping an eye on her. The woman's dress though, also made of animal hide, revolted Appdev.

The sentry viewed Appdev's unexpected jerk not with alarm, but as a signal. She ran out through the tent flap to alert her superior.

A moment later, the guard reappeared with another woman, this one garbed in a flower-print cotton dress. Appdev had grown fond of cotton on Earth. It was a lot like acrylic, which is what she wore a lot of back home.

Neither of these Earth women spoke. Appdev decided not to try to engage them. They were the enemy and Candorians like her were notoriously bad at keeping secrets.

As the guard kept Appdev sighted over a rifle barrel, the other woman cut the twine from the officer's wrists and ankles. Appdev felt the blood flowing again, first with dullness, then irritation, then pain, then normality. The woman in the floral dress offered her a garment, which Appdev accepted with, at first, great enthusiasm.

That the garment was made from animal skin, rather than faux acrylic, dimmed her enthusiasm. When she put it on, she noticed how short it was cut and that dimmed her enthusiasm further.

When she was bound again at gunpoint in only slightly less restricting knots, her enthusiasm was quashed altogether.

General Camille Dishinstaller instant-messaged her staff in Palm Springs explaining, in code, that there must now be a truce between America's Well Regulated Militia and the forces of the Eminent Domain. All hostilities must cease so they could unite against the Terrahist threat. A combined force would form in Las Vegas. Ground troops were to muster at Spaceport Friendliness, where they could be supported by a Domestic airlift wing and armored troops.

"Should we inform President Cox-Arquette?" asked duty officer Lieutenant Gates Branchmanager.

"No rush," Dishinstaller replied. "Well, if he asks."

☆☆☆

President Sajak Pickfour's imminent arrival took the Oops Doctrine off the table.

So General Sanmateo Veecey had to explain it three times to his new adjutant, whose sole qualifications for the job were that he was already part of the headquarters staff, he was recovering well from his bout with fast food and, he wasn't surnamed Daytrader. Eventually, the aide got the picture. While he, Veecey, took a short furlough, he was ceding command to an obscure Friends Helping Friends officer, who looked like Camille Dishinstaller, sounded like Camille Dishinstaller, answered to 'Camille Dishinstaller,' but couldn't possibly be her. Still, Domestic ground forces were to take orders from her or any officers designated by her, no matter how American they looked.

More qualifications on the part of Veecey's new aide would have been nice, but could not have prevented the bloodshed that followed. Veecey had to take responsibility for that. He could blame the omission on his recent bouts of irregular sleep, which would have been the flimsiest of excuses. Because, in his orders, he had specified only ground troops – forgetting he had also committed a flight of shuttles to move troops and tanks to the landing zone in Dakota – the aide passed the orders to the infantry only.

☆☆☆

President Sajak Pickfour of the Eminent Domain surveyed the destruction east of Modesto. The charred remains of a once-pristine forest stretched farther than the eye could see.

Pickfour's face, recorded for posterity by a hovering galacticam drone, was grim. To his right and a step behind was Ambassador Ziglar Tobaccoflack, who had ensconced himself as the president's constant companion. M. Griffin Croupier VII, whom Tobaccoflack succeeded when he was demoted to his post in America, was not with them. There had been a perfunctory meeting at the spaceport on the way in, when Pickfour made it clear he didn't have time for losers.

So less than an hour later, Croupier was back at his duties as America's viceroy and Pickfour was standing on the edge of the charred gorge in central California.

The president gritted his teeth as he spoke: "Yo, Semite."

Other members of his entourage tried to mask quizzical looks.

"Sir," Tobaccoflack offered, "I think they pronounce it, 'Yo-semitty'."

"You say tomato, I say potato," the president replied. "This isn't at all how I pictured America, Ziggy. You know, last time we visited, we stayed in the capital, never got to see the country."

"There's less and less country to see every day, Sir."

"And that's a crying shame, Zig. I always imagined America to be a land of freckle-faced boys, pigtailed girls, mothers in aprons and fathers who smoked a pipe. Like out of an old painting by George Lincoln Rockwell."

"If you say so, Mister President."

☆☆☆

The elite squad headed by Gunnery Sergeant Chuck-Claude Spamblocker was billeted in the Bellagio's Donatello Room, where, with great intensity, they were concentrating on their pre-mission checklist. That involved inspecting their gear, cleaning it, then inspecting it again. But they sprang to attention as their mentor and longtime commanding officer, Lieutenant Colonel Sanjay Sanchez, stepped into the room. His checklist had been completed and he stood before them in battle dress, every inch the professional warrior.

Spamblocker roared a guttural directive that sounded as if it had the same etymological root as 'Attention!'

"At ease," the colonel replied, when all but the gunny returned to their business.

"Good to have you back, Sir," Spamblocker said, speaking for the unit. "It hasn't been the same since they kicked you upstairs."

"Good to be going back out on a mission," the officer admitted. "Don't let this get back to the general, because it's got nothing to do with her personally, or professionally. It's just that staff work was driving me crazy."

"Will you be leading this operation?"

"Yes, Gunny," Sanchez said. "General Dishinstaller will stay in the rear. On the ground, I've got seniority over Colonel Celltower, so I'll have tactical command.

"What about General Veecey, Sir?" Spamblocker asked. "After all, this is a joint op."

"He's got a specific role to play in the battle plan, so he agreed to cede operational authority to me," Sanchez said. "Besides, his troops aren't in fighting shape right now, so he'll be relying on us being able to work seamlessly."

☆☆☆

Unnoticed by the American troops, M. Griffin Croupier VII waited just outside the door, listening in. He longed for that kind of camaraderie. Listening to the officer brief his trusted sergeant, hearing the mutual admiration in their voices, reminded Croupier of how lonely he truly was.

He was keenly aware that the reason the Americans didn't notice him was not because he was stealthily eavesdropping on privileged information. He was, after all, present when the battle plan was formed. The only reason the troops didn't notice him was because, in their estimation, he didn't matter.

The recently promoted Lieutenant Colonel G.Q. Celltower brushed past Croupier with a distracted "Scuze me," and walked through the door, where he was afforded the same ritual as Sanchez.

"You still owe us each a beer," Spamblocker said to the intelligence officer he had known since childhood, "Sir."

"And I'll pay up after this mission, Chuckie," Celltower said. "In the meantime, I have to admit that you guys are better soldiers than I am a spy."

"What's all that about, G.Q.?" Sanchez asked.

"Before the invasion, I used to practice evasion with

these guys while they were practicing ambush techniques," Celltower replied. "Kept us all sharp."

Croupier yearned for a male with whom to bond.

☆☆☆

"Do you know who I am?" the old woman asked Captain Iman Appdev.

"No," she replied coldly, sitting in the farthest corner of the tepee, to the extent tepees might have corners.

"I have been given the name Fire from the Lake."

"I am sorry that your parents hated you so much."

"The entire tribe gave me this name, as they gave me the authority of Peace Chief."

"Peace Chief sounds like a do-nothing job right about now."

Fire from the Lake smiled.

"For now, child. But not for long, we hope. We will hold you only until our demands are met."

"I know all about your demands and the Eminent Domain will never meet them," Appdev stated with defiance. "We'll leave this ball of dirt but only when the threat you pose is neutralized. And we will never, ever bow to people like you."

"People like me?"

"Who say that Earth is better than any other planet just because humanity has been here longer. We've done pretty well for ourselves out in the galaxy. I'd suggest you come out and visit, but you might blow something else up."

"Are you always so forthright?"

"Yes," the Candorian-raised Appdev said, "and I hope it annoys the shit out of you."

TREACHERY

It was a far different Bellagio from when Friends Helping Friends set up headquarters there. People given to hyperbole might say that it looked like a war zone. It didn't. The grand hotel-turned-executive-mansion was surrendered almost without a fight during the invasion and had been spared further degradation throughout the insurgency.

It wasn't structurally unsound. It wasn't even pockmarked by weapons' fire. It was, however, shabby.

There was a sense of decay about the place. Wallpaper, scuffed and damaged through the course of regular wear and tear, remained on the wall because replacements weren't available. Mirrored and brass surfaces needed polishing, but no help was available to take on the task. Water stains mottled the carpet. The mold that caught hold in those spots emitted odors that were growing progressively worse.

Up on the fourth floor, the Donatello room was buzzing with activity as the staging for the raid continued. Gunny Spamblocker and his troops continued to check and re-check their weapons and ask each other questions about the mission in an oral drill to make sure nobody forgot any details.

General Dishinstaller and Colonel Sanchez went over the

strategy. General Veecey and Colonel Celltower discussed their part in the plan, putting their jealousies aside for the moment.

The cacophony was becoming too much for M. Griffin Croupier VII. So was the marginalization.

"Hey!" he shouted over the din. "Hey! Could someone explain something to me?"

Things quieted down, even though Croupier could tell he had nobody's complete attention. Everyone still seemed to be going down their checklists.

"I just want to make sure I got this straight," he said. "I looked over the plan. General Veecey is going to be in this battle, but not in a command capacity. He'll be equal partners with Colonel Celltower."

There were nods.

"Dishinstaller, an American general, will have command of an army comprised, in the main, of Domestic troops but, we're hoping to not need them."

Nods again.

"Colonel Sanchez has operational authority but, because we're depending on the stealth of a small elite unit, Gunny Spamblocker will have tactical control."

"So what's confusing you?" Veecey asked Croupier.

"It looks like everything's getting done," Croupier pointed out, "but nobody's really in charge."

Dishinstaller, Sanchez, Celltower, Spamblocker and each of the five enlisted troops ceased whatever tasks they were attending to, turned to face Croupier and announced, in chorus, "Welcome to America!"

Then they all went back to work.

Veecey escorted his civilian friend out, suggesting he go take a walk.

Croupier did take a walk. A long one.

Feeling ineffectual, feeling frustrated, feeling sorry for

himself, he just kept putting one foot in front of another until he had followed the Strip as far south as it went. Then he just kept on walking, unaware of his surroundings and without the company of his security guards - who were increasingly flabby and useless from too much edible garbage.

He didn't even realize how far he'd walked until he passed under the crumbling relic of an archway that had once supported Interstate 215. He hadn't even noticed how dark it had become and how few streetlights were functioning, nor how many streetlights were rendered non-functional by people who didn't want to be seen.

Now that he realized how far he had walked, he was past caring. He continued to trudge on past Warm Springs Road.

Bored with walking in a straight line, he hung a soft right onto Blue Diamond.

☆☆☆

By coincidence, Gene and Bertie had just decided to turn left onto Blue Diamond. But they weren't on foot.

They had been waiting for the cover of darkness to test-drive a conveyance that, although it was assembled from scrap from countless models of armored vehicles that had been lying around the desert for untold years, most resembled on the outside an M1A2 Abrams main battle tank. There were fifty more of them penned up in the warehouse, almost ready to roll in support of the coming attack on the Terrahists.

This particular tank, though, would one day soon roll into glory. But that night, it was heading straight for Croupier.

☆☆☆

Croupier heard them long before they saw him and using discretion, decided to keep walking, casually, hoping he wouldn't be spotted by the rapidly approaching death machine. Lacking proper training, he didn't know that walking, casually, was a poor tactical choice when in that situation, compared with cowering, nervously.

On the periphery of his vision, he could see a warehouse's barn-sized doors, open, revealing a well-lit nest of finished, battle-ready tanks, a few welders' arcs putting the last few together and a regiment of American soldiers ready to drive them off.

Before there was an insurgency, there was the Well Regulated Militia. Before there was the Militia, there was the 3rd Armored Cavalry Regiment. Gene, Bertie and the soldiers in that warehouse, considered themselves the spiritual descendants of the men who stormed Santa Ana's palace, opened the Oregon Trail and spearheaded Patton's assault on the Rhineland.

Acting nonchalant was all Croupier had, and it wasn't nearly enough.

☆☆☆

The interior of the tank was less impressive than its exterior. Times being what they were, the insurgency couldn't spare the resources to fully complement a four-man tank, so the two veteran soldiers had to take out all the electronic gear that made the Abrams distinctive. While Bertie drove, Gene rode in the turret and fired the weapon. It was more like a 60-ton Sherman with a 120-millimeter gun.

One thing all armored vehicles through history had in common though, was that it was very loud in there.

"Hey, Gene!" Bertie shouted over the din. "Got your night goggles on? You see that little fella?"

"Yes, I do, Bertie! Ought he to be all the way out here?"

"Not while we're trying to keep an entire tank base a secret! Can't run the risk he's with the Terrahists! Fire!"

☆☆☆

The remnants of the 3rd Cav weren't about to waste a 120-millimeter shell on one skinny civilian.

Automatic weapon rounds, though, were another story.

M. Griffin Croupier VII was mowed down like a row of Kansas wheat.

☆☆☆

"Hey, Gene!" Bertie shouted. "You watch the news? You know who that looked like?"

"Now that you mention it!"

Then, in unison, they summed up the whole situation: "Oops."

☆☆☆

All this took place within sight of a Domestic shuttle crew taking off from the nearby spaceport. A crew that never received General Veecey's orders that it was now, for all practical purposes, under American command.

"Cap, is that a tank?" the puffy-faced co-pilot asked the woman sitting in the left-hand seat. He took one more bite of his cheeseburger.

"Sure is, Sparky," the pilot replied. "And it's one of theirs."

"How can you be sure?"

She gave him a long look before reminding him, "Because we don't have any. Put down that burger. We're going in!"

Cargo shuttles like hers were unarmed, but Gene and Bertie had no way of knowing that. They turned tail and headed into the desert.

"Wouldya look at that?" the pilot wondered, as she caught a glimpse through the rapidly closing doors to the warehouse. "Must be a whole troop or more in there."

"What are we gonna do, Cap?"

"All we can. First we're going to check to see if that poor guy down there is still alive," she replied, then spoke into her comnet link, "Tower, this is cargo two-two-seven. Returning with injured passenger. Request medic standing by. Further request aerial bombardment, repeat ..."

Within five minutes, Croupier was being treated by the best team of battlefield surgeons ever assembled, and the warehouse as well as its materiel and personnel were completely obliterated.

Within those five minutes, Bertie, Gene and their tank, the last vestige of the 3rd Cav, swung around to the east-northeast and roared off at the maximum speed of forty miles an hour in the direction of Dakota.

As long as the Brave Rifles of the 3rd Cav could field one piece of armor, they'd make do. Even if the Domestic hover-trailers, that were powerful enough to carry an entire column of tanks thirteen hundred miles to make their rendezvous, could no longer be counted on, they'd find a way into the fight, or make a way.

Orders were orders.

"We'll never make it in time!" Gene shouted.

"We'll make it! We'll make it!" Bertie replied.

But, at forty miles an hour, it would take them thirty-three hours if they drove straight through. Plus gas stops.

If Bertie was right, there wasn't a second to spare.

☆☆☆

Iman Appdev was getting used to leather.

Still, she was glad to have it removed from her wrists as she sat in the tepee across from Fire from the Lake, under heavy guard of course.

"We really mean you no harm," the Peace Chief told the Domestic officer.

"Yeah, well you certainly harmed enough people on MetLifeWorld and HomeDepotWorld," Appdev retorted.

The old Terrahist was moved by that.

"We did what was necessary," she said.

"Necessary for what? To bring a three-million-strong army into a shootout on this world you say you love so much? To have your own people setting torch to your forests?"

"The Mother has great powers to heal herself," came the patient reply. "All that happened was our exact intention."

"Then your intention must be suicide."

"No doubt it looks that way to you."

Appdev, furious to the point of not caring about the Raysprayer pointed at her, rose up and paced around the tent. Fire from the Lake permitted this, although the guard's vigilance was heightened.

"Then explain this to me! Why are you doing this?" Appdev asked. Then, her internal filter permanently disabled, she added, "I want to know why I'm here."

"The army of sky soldiers is here because we brought them to eliminate our greatest rival for dominion over this half of the Mother World."

"You knew that we'd blame Barber?"

"Your chief and the westerners' chief are great enemies. That is what happens when two men can no longer be great friends."

That Sajak Pickfour and Watts Barber were even casual acquaintances was news to Appdev.

"We knew," the Terrahist chief continued, "that your chief would believe what he wanted to believe. We would be rid of our enemy and the star soldiers would someday return to the stars."

Appdev stood there in silence, trying to grasp it all.

"That is why the sky soldiers are here," Fire from the Lake concluded. "Only you can answer why you are among them."

☆☆☆

A calm had settled over the Donatello Room as the officers and elite troops waited for the transport that would send them into the fray. With Domestic technology at their disposal, the trip would take mere minutes.

Of course, the transport was late. Some snafu at the

spaceport, they were told.

The boredom was broken when Veecey's comnet transceiver beeped.

"Veecey here," he said then, a moment later, turned deathly pale.

"What is it, Veecey?" Dishinstaller asked. "What's gone wrong?"

"Griff Croupier's been hit, he's fighting for his life on an operating table," Veecey seethed.

"How did this happen?" Sanchez asked. "I gave an order to cooperate in full with all Domestic authorities and got responses from one hundred percent of my field commanders."

"Knew I could count on you," Dishinstaller said.

"Only have to tell me once," Sanchez said. "Of course, there is that fog of war. Anything could've happened out there, but it would've been an error, not enemy action."

"How about you, Veecey?" Dishinstaller asked. "When you switched enemies, did you send out a memo?"

He had, but couldn't be sure, given the size of the military bureaucracy underneath him, that everyone had signed off.

"Put everything on hold until tomorrow," he said as he rushed out of the door, along the hall and down the fire stairs. "I'm going to the hospital!"

"Veecey!" Dishinstaller called out after him. "What about Pickfour?"

"Shit!" Veecey said and halted in his tracks. Pickfour and that turd Tobaccoflack would require some kind of official media op of a send-off, before they'd get on the shuttle to take them up to their transport and be on their way. And it wouldn't do to have them involved in the mess he was cooking up at that moment.

"Celltower!" he called out. "Get to the spaceport. Pretend you're somebody important. Kiss the president's ass and get him on his flight!"

☆☆☆

Sunrise Hospital had gone very much to seed during Watts Barber's reign as America's president, although it was reinvigorated when the Eminent Domain's military came to Las Vegas and converted the hospital into its première trauma center.

General Sanmateo Veecey spent long hours in the waiting room, sipping horrid coffee, hoping that he was sending enough positive vibes into the universe to save his friend.

☆☆☆

"Do I know you, son?" the president asked the tall, decorous but disheveled man in casual clothes, who was there to represent Friends Helping Friends.

"No, Sir, but I'm a big fan," G.Q. Celltower replied. The president wasn't buying it. "And contributor."

Ah, the magic word, he thought as the president's demeanor brightened.

"Where's Lucky?"

"It's on Fremont Street, Sir."

"The president meant Mister Croupier, not the hotel, young man," Tobaccoflack clarified. "What's Mister Croupier doing now?"

Celltower then realized he had been spying on Griff Croupier for almost three years now, and still struggled to understand what he did. *Think, G.Q.! What does an administrator do all day?*

"Oh, he's being very proactive in forming an opportunity matrix for leveraging all resources in a bleeding-edge process to more effectively win the peace."

It sounded like complete bullshit to Celltower. It sounded like complete bullshit to Tobaccoflack too and, for that matter, to the president.

"That's what I'm paying him for." Pickfour said. "Tell him we said 'hey.' C'mon, Zig, we got a flight to catch."

☆☆☆

An indeterminate period of bright fluorescence, dull tile, molded plastic and gleaming metal passed. Veecey continued to fight fatigue.

"Could you use some company?" a husky voice behind him called.

"Hmm? Oh, hi, Dishinstaller."

"You OK?"

"As well as can be expected."

"I wish I could say the same," the American commander said. "It's 'Mat,' right? Mat, things are worse than we thought. As fond as I'm sure you are of your friend in there, we got a bigger problem. In retribution, your people took out our entire armored force."

"All of it?"

"Everything that was in our warehouse near McCarran. We're presuming that's everything. You want to scrub the mission?"

Veecey thought for a second.

"Well, the tanks were pretty much just our backup plan," he figured. "No, we're good to go."

"Agreed, Mat. Don't know why our intel people keep telling us you're the most indecisive, amateurish general officer in the galaxy."

"They're being kind," Veecey admitted. "I'm not cut out for this. If I get back alive from this, I'm hanging up my uniform. Retire. Maybe teach."

"What field?"

"American music," Veecey said. "I got a great collection ..." he started, then realized he might say too much. She'd be within her rights to shoot him as a looter.

"Don't worry. I put it there."

"You did?"

"Yeah. It was a honey pot to keep you distracted. We knew you loved music. Weren't sure how you felt about girls, but we knew you loved music."

"It worked," Veecey said then asked, after a pause, "How did you know about that? Celltower?"

"Naaah. Believe it or not, his best stuff got lost in the mail. We actually got that from the Terrahists."

Veecey's eyes widened.

"So there was a connection between the Barber regime and the perpetrators of When All Hell ..."

"Calm down. No. Some people I knew from high school tipped me off. If I knew where they were calling from, I'd tell you, I swear on my honor. The connection doesn't go higher or deeper."

"But the question then," Veecey said, suddenly re-energized, "is where did *they* get *their* information from?"

"That is a very good question."

"What else did you get out of them?"

"The coordinates for your first landfall. That there was nothing more to your Astonishment Campaign than a fancy light show. That ..."

"Astonishment, I want to tell you, wasn't my idea. It was cooked up way above my pay grade. It was the best I could do with the rules of engagement I was handed from Admiral Daytrader, and they were forced down his throat by ... by ..."

"Yeah?"

Veecey paused a moment. Yes, before this business began, he was shunted off to the least critical commands because he tended to put off making choices until compelled to, giving him a reputation for being 'indecisive.' It was a word Admiral Daytrader had used in his performance reviews. And yet Daytrader promoted him and gave him command of the American invasion on the insistence of ...

"Tobaccoflack!"

Veecey contacted the spaceport's control tower via comnet.

"This is Veecey! Stop the president's shuttle! Take Ambassador Tobaccoflack off the craft and hold him under whatever pretenses! ... Already? Damn! ... Well, patch me through to his transport. Now! ... Veecey here! Who's this? ... Nealon, this is an urgent security matter of the utmost national importance: Place Ziglar Tobaccoflack under arrest for treason! ... Yes, you read me? Do it now!"

☆☆☆

The burly, thick-necked man known to President Sajak Pickfour as Nealon was the most trusted member of his protection service. Unknown to the president, Ambassador Ziglar Tobaccoflack trusted him even more. And Nealon was as addicted to trust as Tobaccoflack was to adulation.

Nealon had intercepted the message. Now he would forget he ever heard it. Problem solved. He would take a nap now.

"Hey, Parnell, I'm going off shift," he told his replacement. "G'night."

"'Night, Nealon," Parnell said as he sat down at the guard desk, between the Exceptional's flight desk and its passenger compartment. "Anything to report?"

"Nope. All quiet."

☆☆☆

"Did you get through?" Dishinstaller asked Veecey.

"Yeah, but the guy I spoke with didn't seem too concerned," Veecey replied. "Either he's an exceptionally cool-headed professional, or President Pickfour is in grave danger."

☆☆☆

Nothing could be further from the truth. While it was, without question, factual to report that Sajak Pickfour was alone in his private cabin with a traitor, that turncoat had no intention of assassinating him. He could do the Mother Earth movement much more good by continuing to manipulate the president.

It wasn't Pickfour who was in trouble. It was the Eminent Domain.

So the two men sat in cushy chairs and sipped from exotically-flavored water with the barest traces of a vodka-like substance infused in it. That was Pickfour's idea, it should be clarified.

"Thank goodness we're off that rock," Pickfour said.

"Oh, I don't know Sir," Tobaccoflack replied. "I don't think Earth's that bad. Of course it'll need some substantial long-term aid packages. It'll cost us a fortune, sure, but we can really make that planet beautiful again."

"Well, we'll see what we can squeeze out of the Archsenate, Zig."

"I know you'll do what you can, Sir."

The president took a long sip of his drink.

"Zig, I do appreciate you coming all the way out here with me. I don't know what I'd do without you."

"It's an honor and a privilege, Mister President."

"Yeah, but all this traveling can wear a fella down."

"That's true, Sir," Tobaccoflack agreed. "But at least it's not like the old days."

The president's relaxed good-fellowship turned into dour suspicion.

"What do you mean, Zig?"

"Well, I mean, way back, when spacecraft couldn't travel faster than light like we can now and it would've taken years to get from the homeworlds to ..."

"Now wait just a second, Mister Tobaccoflack," the president said with unaccustomed formality. "I'm a rock-ribbed, dyed-in-the-wool Einsteinian."

"Yes, Sir, I know."

The whole galaxy knew Sajak Pickfour's religious convictions.

"Albert Einstein said that faster-than-light travel is impossible. It's true. And I believe it."

"Of course, Sir, but how do you explain ..."

"I leave it to my sciences advisors to figure out how it's done, but I know in my heart that this ship cannot really, in truth, travel faster than light."

Tobaccoflack could feel the air being sucked out of the room. Metaphorically, of course, but he knew that he'd be finding out what it was like, literally, in short order. He had one chance: to argue with a religious zealot until he changed his mind. That is, he had no chance at all.

"But Sir, you can't argue with the evidence of your own ..."

"Nealon!" he called into the comnet box on the bulkhead. *Yes*, thought Tobaccoflack. *Nealon. Good ol' Nealon.*

"Nealon's on a break, Sir," came the squawk out of the box. "This is Parnell. Anything I can do for you?"

"Could you escort the ambassador to the airlock like a good fella?"

The transport landed on the lawn of Pickfour's palace a short time later - and Pickfour wasted no effort on understanding why the time was so short - with one passenger fewer.

The Domestic law enforcement authorities, though, had a field day with the decedent's trunk full of fan mail from Earth.

Some of it was sweet. Some of it was explicit. Most of it used the phrase 'Mother Earth' somewhere in the text. Other personal papers implicated Nealon, whose fate was not as swift as Tobaccoflack's.

It took less than one pay period for a made-for-galacticam movie about the epic struggle aboard the president's transport to be produced and broadcast. The life-and-death struggle between the crafty darling of the mainstream media and the ideologically pure president was, by that telling, fought with laser pistols, daggers and finally hand-to-hand. Time was compressed to a more dramatic demonstration of the treachery of Nealon, who was recast as a very attractive woman with expensive tastes in lingerie.

The pay period after that was the presidential election. Polls taken before the president's last trip to Earth showed that he was in deep trouble with the voters but, in the warm glow of the galacticam movie, Sajak Pickfour was re-elected with ease.

BATTLE

The doctor pulled off her surgical mask as she entered the waiting room.

"General Veecey? Is that General Dishinstaller with you? I never imagined I'd meet the two of you at the ..."

"How is he, doc?" Veecey cut in as he got to his feet.

"I'll level with you. He lost a lot of blood. We had to remove his spleen. His internal ..."

"When's the part where you level with me?"

"He'll pull through. We can keep him alive on meds and a careful diet until all the organs that failed can be cloned. The shuttle crew got him here just in time."

"So he'll be all right?"

The surgeon shook her head.

"He developed a complication. You're a military man. Maybe you've heard of it: the technical term is post-traumatic stress disorder."

It didn't ring a bell with Veecey. Dishinstaller had heard of it but stayed out of it. This wasn't her conversation.

"It used to be called battle fatigue," the surgeon continued.

"Shell shock?"

"Knock off the medical lingo, doc. What's wrong with Griff?"

"He suffers from what is popularly called 'existential

angst'."

"Angst!" Veecey shouted. "No! Is there any hope for him?"

"He'll need counseling. And rest. He can't stay here. You have to send him home."

Veecey didn't technically have the authority to do that, although he promised the surgeon he'd make the arrangements.

"Can I see him?" Veecey asked. The doctor nodded. "I'll be right back, Camille."

Veecey expected to find his friend in a private room, as befitted his station as the emissary of the Eminent Domain. At the very least, he should have been behind a curtain. But there he was, parked on a gurney out in the hall.

Then he looked around at the scores of courageous soldiers – soldiers under his command – who took up all the beds in all the rooms and behind all the curtains and some of whom were also stacked up in hallways.

And they deserved no less.

Veecey strode over to the gurney holding the patient chart referred to as "CROUPIER 7, MERV G."

"Hi, Griff," Veecey said, forcing a smile. "You really gave us a scare."

"It's useless, you know," Croupier said. "We unite with the Militia to fight the Terrahists. Soon another bad actor will come along and we'll unite with the Terrahists to fight them. It's an endless cycle."

"Hey, it's not your problem anymore," Veecey said, trying to cheer him up. "You got angst. One of the first things you learn as a military officer: you can get men to fight with one arm, on one leg, bleeding out of their bellies. But they can't fight when they got angst. It's the only ticket home anymore."

"Great. Like I've got anything to go home to. I'll be a lump on a bed someplace with a little less gravity is all."

And then he began sobbing uncontrollably, choking on his

words. Veecey didn't understand much of the rest of what Croupier said, except that his ex-husband's name was Steve.

A nurse, mercifully, injected Croupier with a sedative and, before drifting off to sleep, he muttered something that made little sense to Veecey, even though the words were more intelligible.

"It's all personal, you know," Croupier said as his eyes began to close. "They've known each other forever. Had a falling out. Daytrader told me. Daytrader told me ..."

Another forced smile and Veecey left, not to see Griff Croupier again for quite some time.

☆☆☆

G.Q. Celltower was one of the first members of the Well Regulated Militia to give up wearing his uniform at the insurgency. Now, full circle, he was one of the last insurgents to put his uniform back on.

He had kept it in a duffel bag under the cot he slept on in a room in a Bellagio sub-basement he shared with eight other hotel employees. He wondered if any of those eight – actually he wondered how many – were also spies.

He strode into the Donatello room wearing it, to the catcalls of Lieutenant Colonel Sanjay Sanchez and his troops.

As the razzing died down, Celltower could hear his childhood pal, Gunnery Sergeant Chuck-Claude Spamblocker, chide, "Nice pants, Galvin. But they make your butt look big."

"First of all, it's 'G.Q.'," Celltower began. "Second, it's 'Sir.' Third, they do not."

"G.Q., I'm sure everyone knows the gunny was joking," Sanchez said. "Let's stay focused on the mission. Galvin, you and General Veecey will – speaking of – attention!"

Generals Veecey and Dishinstaller arrived at that point.

"At ease, everyone," Veecey said, with uncharacteristic terseness. "Celltower, our shuttle's waiting. Everyone else, good luck. See you in Dakota."

They left for the spaceport and didn't exchange another word until they were in position.

"As you were," Dishinstaller said to the grizzled colonel.

"We'll be following in ten minutes," Sanchez said, addressing the half dozen enlisted men and women. "Remember, the Domestic troops are exhausted, ailing, injured and barely battle-ready. Don't gloat. You're the best we got and I don't know what you six would look like after three years on an alien world. More to the point, it means that our infantry support will be minimal. The general will scrape together what she can. As you all know by now, we can't expect tank support at all. With a little luck, though, the weather will hold and we'll at least have air support courtesy of the Domestic Armada."

☆☆☆

Luck was with them. It was a bright summer day over Dakota. There wasn't a cloud in the sky. The forecast for the week called for nothing but brilliant sunshine.

But there's such a thing as too much luck.

Plenty of sun can mean, under unfortunate circumstances, plenty of sunspots. And that kind of activity, combined with the impurities in the American air, played havoc on the Domestic shuttles.

At least twenty miles before the drop-off point, the hovercraft heaved and pitched. The American soldiers were shaken but too proud to show it. Then it happened again and the shuttle pilot put his passengers' safety ahead of their pride.

"Colonel, I have to set it down here," the pilot said.

"Come on, Commander, we're almost there," Sanchez argued. "Tough it out."

"Tell you what," the Domestic pilot countered. "I'm going to touch down right now. Then you show me how tough you and your people are by humping it the rest of the way."

Two minutes later, Sanchez and the squad had their boots

on the ground and were slogging their way north and east, while the shuttle limped along at low altitude and quarter speed back to Las Vegas.

Sanchez got on the comnet badge Veecey had issued him and called.

"Yeah," Veecey replied. "Same thing happened to us. We're on foot going the last thirty klicks."

"Klicks?" Sanchez inquired.

"Kilometers."

"Half-miles," Celltower interjected.

"We got a little farther to go," Sanchez said. "Suggest you hole up for about two hours once you're in position."

"Copy that," Veecey said. "Puts us way behind schedule. The plan was to do this at nightfall, not two in the morning. You know how suspicious that's going to look?"

"Can't be helped, Sir," Sanchez replied, "It's either that or wait another day. But we have a bigger problem."

"What's that?"

"Sunspots are sure to ground General Dishinstaller's shuttles. How are we getting back?"

☆☆☆

Back in Las Vegas, General Camille Dishinstaller hadn't yet heard about the disabled shuttles. She was busy cobbling together a task force out of any able-bodied troops she could find from either the Domestic or American forces to back up Sanchez's vanguard.

Pickings were slim.

The Domestic troops had lost their edge. Cheeseburgers had poisoned their bodies and souls. Victory delayed and denied had demoralized them.

Her own troops, though in better fighting shape, were not as numerous as she had supposed. As she sipped a cola in a departure lounge at the airfield she still knew as McCarran, she wondered what happened to all the soldiers she had ordered to surrender so they could be disarmed, amnestied, re-armed with more technologically-advanced weaponry and defect back to the Militia.

It came to her in a flash.

At the last moment, she realized many, if not most, of them defected to the Terrahist side. She leaned forward and held her head in her hands.

"Ma'am?" a familiar voice queried.

"Yes, son?"

"Lieutenant Branchmanager reporting for duty."

"Welcome to the fight, Gates," she said. "Great to see you out here."

"Great to be out from behind the desk," he replied. "Just want to return the favor, General. All the confidence Colonel Sanchez has always shown in me."

"Get on the shuttle, Lieutenant," she said with a smile.

"Yes, Ma'am," he said, but hesitated. "Ma'am?"

"What?"

"Is it true what they say? Did Croupier crack up?"

"He's suffering from existential angst."

"What's that, Ma'am?"

"It's what we call Woody Allen Syndrome."

"Ooh," he exhaled. "Poor guy."

"It happens, Lieutenant. But don't you worry about it. As long as you stay focused on your job and don't go thinking about the human condition or the universe or your place in it, you'll come through OK."

"Thank you, General."

"Now, why don't you get on your shuttle? Meet your troops."

With a snap to attention and a salute, Branchmanager turned on his heel and marched down to the gate where the Domestic shuttle was waiting for him.

Stepping through the hatch, he saw them all lined up: the soldiers he was to lead into battle.

At first they were all a sea of red shirts. Then he glanced at their faces. To begin with, he thought they all just wore the same sad, resigned expression. Then, on closer inspection, he saw that many of them, in reality, had the same face, differing only in the degree to which they had acquired jowls. Looking into that face over and over again, Lieutenant Gates Branchmanager of America's Well Regulated Militia came to know a flash of existential angst.

But that was OK, he thought, that was external. This was somebody else's angst, not his. This was the angst of people who were bred to be disposable, born to be war casualties.

That wasn't him. He wasn't one of them. No. He was an American. His only connection to these red-shirted wretches was that he was their new platoon leader.

Oh.

That meant he was the one expected to stand between them and whoever was shooting at them.

He wondered, in passing, whatever became of their last platoon leader.

And then Second Lieutenant Gates Branchmanager truly understood existential angst.

☆☆☆

Veecey and Celltower hid themselves behind the same small sand hill on the edge of the Terrahist settlement. From their vantage point they could see no permanent structures, just a city of tents crisscrossed by dirt roads, traveled by dusty internal combustion vehicles.

They didn't compare notes, though. On the pretense of maintaining noise discipline, they spent the next several hours not saying a word to each other.

☆☆☆

General Camille Dishinstaller's neck, ears and nostrils were turning red.

"What do you mean?" she demanded of the pilot of the lead shuttle of the wing that would transport her and her troops to Dakota.

"Sunspots, Ma'am," he said with a shrug. It bothered the general that this flyboy was sitting down, calm and strapped in, but not too securely, munching on chicken nuggets. "Can't go anywhere 'til they clear up. We've lost contact with the two shuttles we already sent."

"How soon can we go?" she asked, reminding herself that this was someone else's military or she'd have shot him already.

"A little after dark," he said with the casualness of someone trying to determine if he's in the mood for honey mustard sauce or sweet-and-sour. "Ask me again once the sun sets."

✭✭✭

"Sanchez, you in position?" Veecey whispered into his comnet badge a few hours later.

"Ready to roll, Sir."

"Good. Let's go do this," the general said, then held his breath as he poured just a drop of chloroform on the back of his field jacket and climbed into G.Q. Celltower's arms.

Celltower carried him over the ridge into the Terrahist camp, then dropped him, without ceremony, at the feet of the first enemy warrior he saw.

"Tell your War Chief," Celltower said, "that the Militia has a gift for him: the War Chief of the star soldiers."

After a thorough frisking that revealed Celltower to be unarmed, the Terrahist warrior and the American spy each grabbed one of Veecey's legs and dragged the general to the tent the Terrahist indicated.

✭✭✭

"We're good to go now, General," the pilot told Camille Dishinstaller, who had taken to boarding the shuttle and heading for the flight deck every two hours since the delays began. "Sunspots have all cleared up."

Dishinstaller thanked him and signaled Branchmanager via

comnet to get the troops off the benches in the departure lounge and back on the shuttle. *Now!*

☆☆☆

"Move out," Sanchez ordered Spamblocker and, by extension, the other five members of the squad as they huddled behind the outermost tepee of the Terrahist settlement.

The gunny hesitated a moment.

"Coming with us, Colonel?"

"Change of plans," Sanchez replied as he pointed to a line of petroleum-powered ground vehicles along the dirt road that approached the camp. "I'm going to find us a lift home. Meet you at the rendezvous point. Luck."

"Luck."

☆☆☆

G.Q. Celltower and the seemingly unconscious Sanmateo Veecey waited in a tepee in the settlement's inner circle. Celltower noticed straightaway that the guard was armed with Domestic weapons – very likely a former Militia member who had joined Croupier's abortive American corps then defected to the Terrahists.

The guard kept a close eye on Celltower. On his hands, Celltower noted, so he obviously had some training. In walked an older, sadder man. This must be the War Chief, Celltower figured, then noticed how the guard didn't react to the headman's presence, but kept staring at his hands, his weapon trained on his chest.

"I am Shoots at the Stars," the War Chief said.

Celltower walked over to him – slowly – thought twice, decided not to offer him a hand to shake, and simply introduced himself, leaving Veecey in a heap on the ground.

"I bring you the leader of the star soldiers to do with as you will," Celltower said, gesturing to Veecey.

"You are a brave warrior for one so good-looking," Shoots

at the Stars said. "What do you seek in return?"

"Your equally good-looking hostage," Celltower said. "Certainly Veecey is more valuable to you."

"Indeed he is."

"So let me take the one called Appdev and I will leave you Veecey."

"What is she to you?" Shoots at the Stars asked.

"I have seduced many women, Great Chief, from many walks of life. I have made them scream. I have made them shout my name into the night, or any of my dozens of aliases. I have made them swoon and I have made them beg. I have had them in beds, on floors, on desks, in department store changing rooms, on life rafts, in church parking lots, in bakery ovens, in the baggage compartments of ..."

"I get the picture," Shoots at the Stars said, to Veecey's relief.

"But Iman Appdev is the only one I have boffed twice in one night and still want to boff again. Return this woman to me, for without her I shall never understand the lust other women feel for me."

"I would say how sweet that was, if I were capable of sarcasm," said Appdev who had suddenly, silently, appeared outside the tent flap.

Veecey sprang up, his ponytail whipping around, and pulled a small device out of his field jacket.

He and Celltower stood shoulder to shoulder. They glanced momentarily - for a moment was more than they could spare - at their mutual object of desire. They shared the same thought, *Wow, she looks hot in a short leather skirt.*

"Appdev, come over here!" Veecey ordered. "We're here to rescue you, then we're all going home."

"Maybe I don't want to be rescued," a voice coming from about a meter above her hemline told Veecey. It was a familiar voice, though unsettlingly serene. "Maybe I *am* home."

"We'll talk about this later," the general said, realizing she was not under guard. Had she been turned? Had she convinced them she had, in order to gain some freedom of action? "Right now, why don't you tell your hosts what I'm holding?"

"It's a Daytrader Industries Annihilation Grenade, Version 2D, Model TXH1131," the woman once known as Iman Appdev replied, with an eerie calmness. "It is a product of DaewooWorld's Production Plant Number ..."

"That's good enough for current purposes," Veecey explained. "What she hasn't got around to telling you yet is that it will level this whole camp, and wipe the faces off that mountain we passed on the way in."

Shoots at the Stars stood, impassive, as his guard kept his Raysprayer trained on Celltower.

Everyone in the tent knew that the pivot in this standoff was Iman Appdev. Where did her loyalties lie? Shoots at the Stars, who felt he had developed a level of trust with the young woman, who had already taken on a Terrahist name, whispered gently to her, "Do what you must, Knees By Her Tits."

And the serene glow vanished from her face. She was again the sworn defender of the Eminent Domain.

"Appdev, take the man's weapon," Veecey ordered.

She hesitated a moment but, in the end, complied.

"Hand it over to Celltower."

"Why? I can handle a weapon as well as either of you."

"But ... but ..." Veecey stammered, "but you're the one being *rescued*!"

Again, she complied but pouted over it.

They stood there for a tense moment. Veecey, Celltower and Appdev on one side of the tepee, the Terrahists on the other.

"Remember your training," Shoots at the Stars advised his young comrade.

Then the two Terrahists fell to the ground, pulled up the nearest tent pins and ran screaming into the night.

Or at least, it sounded to Domestic ears like screaming. It was really the Sioux war cry: *Ai-ee-yah!*

☆☆☆

Ai-ee-yah was co-opted in the 19th century by the Sioux's fiercest enemies and espoused as their own war cry.

Those enemies were the Brave Rifles of the 3rd Cavalry Regiment.

At that moment, the regiment's sole remaining vehicle had passed Mount Rushmore and was within eyeshot of the camp. Gene and Bertie were, at that moment, screaming *Ai-ee-yah* as well.

☆☆☆

Gunnery Sergeant Chuck-Claude Spamblocker and his unit had located the one semi-permanent structure in the tent city. Spamblocker assumed at first that it was a meeting room or feasting hall or perhaps a store room. It turned out to be the latrine, but still. A defensible position was a defensible position.

Veecey, Celltower and Appdev emerged from the collapsed tent and saw Spamblocker waving them over. They ran, weaving across a hail of Raysprayer and shotgun fire, for the door the gunny held open. They each dove in headfirst and slid along the floor. Pretending to toughness they didn't feel, they all refused to say *eeeewwww.* Spamblocker's squad took up positions at each window.

"Are you OK, Iman?" Celltower asked, shouting over the chaos of the ensuing firefight.

Damn, Veecey thought. *I wanted to be the first to ask.*

"As if you care," Appdev said, noticing that eye contact with the handsome American was not to be had. "I'll save you the trouble, Porsche or G.Q. or whatever your name is. I *am* wearing panties."

"I knew you would," Veecey said, sensing an opportunity to regain the offensive and ignoring an annoying beep from his comnet badge. "When we get back to the Eminent Domain, I'll make sure you have whatever kind of wardrobe you ever imagined yourself in. You'll be the toast of ..."

"I'll be a trophy, Mat," Appdev said, a fat blur of a projectile smashing through the wall and sailing by her, missing her throat by an inch. "That's not what I was brought up to be."

That beep again.

"So what is it you want? Look at all I have to offer you, Iman," Veecey went on.

"Begging the General's pardon," Spamblocker said, slipping a power pack into his Raysprayer as if it were the most precious thing in his life, "but would you mind answering that hail? Might be important, Sir."

"About damn time," General Camille Dishinstaller's husky voice called out of the comnet badge. "Mat, what's your position?"

"We're in a wooden structure at the center of camp," Veecey replied. "Can you see us?"

"Affirm. Stay put," Dishinstaller ordered. "It looks like there's only one squad exchanging fire with you. The main Terrahist force has regrouped at the north end of the camp. We're going to land at the south end. Wait for our signal and make your way toward us. Copy?"

"Copy."

At the end of that exchange, Spamblocker asked, "Any idea when that signal's going to come, Sir?"

"No, Gunny, I didn't ask. Why?"

"Well, Sir, we're not equipped for a pitched battle," Spamblocker explained. "We're going to be running out of ammo soon."

If Lieutenant Colonel Sanjay Sanchez had been party to that

conversation, he'd have survived.

Instead, under the conservative but mistaken assumption that rescue was not coming, he was busy stealing a van.

It was a cargo van, not built for passengers. But it would fit his entire team and comfort was the least of their concerns.

The battle-hardened officer was an old hand at all manner of war craft. Hotwiring an internal combustion engine was second nature to him. However, he knew nothing about Domestic intra-atmosphere shuttles or how sunspots affected them, or that the problem would solve itself as long as day continued to turn into night.

He had no way of knowing that.

But not checking the contents of the back of the van was a fatal mistake.

That wasn't just any van. To Should Switch to Decaf and Stuffed in a Gym Locker, it was home.

They were sound asleep when the shooting started. They weren't bolted awake until their bedrolls slid hard into the back doors as Sanjay Sanchez peeled out.

When the van slammed through the latrine's western wall, almost crushing a member of Spamblocker's unit, it was with Sanchez's bloodied body at the wheel, the exit wound of a pistol shot obscuring all features above the bridge of his nose.

Aghast, nobody in the small, noisome hut noticed the clanking outside, or that the weapons' fire outside had stopped abruptly.

The two men who climbed over their revered colonel's body and onto the hood of the van were flush with firepower, as their rapid-fire assault rifle shots over the team's heads attested.

"Drop your weapons!" demanded Should Switch to Decaf, pointing his rifle at Spamblocker. "You too! You too!" he repeated for everyone else there. "You imperialist dogs!" he shouted at Veecey and Appdev. "You traitorous scum!" he shouted at the rest. "The Mother Earth movement has grown stronger as a result of your conflict and is destined to emerge victorious! We will watch you dig your graves and we will bury you alive in them, even though interment in the Great Mother herself is too good for you! And to ensure that flowering plants will emerge from you carcasses, I will personally squat down on your graves and squeeze out a ..."

"Deke, don't you think we should just kill them and rejoin our forces?" Stuffed in a Gym Locker asked. "I mean, their friends can't be far behind. We have to brace ourselves for an all-out assault."

"In a minute, Gym, right now I'm on a roll," Deke replied with a little less volume, but went right back into rant mode. "Where was I? Oh yes! I will squeeze out a six-inch-thick, two-pound pile of ..."

"Shit!" screamed Gym. But he hadn't really been listening; instead, he was reacting to what felt like an earthquake.

The van was crushed under the half-track of the hollowed-out shell of an Abrams tank. So was the body of Sanjay Sanchez, but so also were the two Terrahist gunmen.

"Are we late?" Gene asked, his broad face and tousled mane popping up from the turret, as Bertie downshifted the tank to muffle it a bit.

"Negative," Spamblocker said. "You're right on time."

"Of course we are," Bertie said, as his bushy eyebrows emerged from the driver's hatch. "We're the Cavalry!"

☆☆☆

There was still the matter of Shoots at the Stars' massed Terrahist army on the one side of camp and Dishinstaller's ragtag, but determined, combined force on the other.

Appdev and her rescuers had fallen back to the southern edge of the camp. Now the two forces inched closer to each other and, in all likelihood, to mutual destruction. Everyone thought they were going to die. Everyone kept advancing anyway, brave souls that they were.

One soul, the bravest, emerged from the mess of tumbled-down tents, waving her arms up and down, suggesting a request for quiet and stillness.

It was Fire from the Lake.

"Let there be an end," was all she said. All she had to say.

The Terrahists of the Mother Earth movement looked around at the barren landscape and realized that, in their zeal to garner respect for the planet they claimed to love, they may have caused it great injury.

The Americans realized they had an opportunity which comes around maybe once every couple of centuries to start over, with a new government and a new covenant between its leaders and its people.

The Domestic troops realized they could now go home with their honor intact.

All was quiet. Somewhere nearby, a small bird found a sapling sturdy enough to support a nest and began singing a joyous song.

Soldiers on all sides safety-locked their weapons, pointed them at the ground, and leaned on them in their exhaustion.

Someone on the Terrahist side cleared his throat to preface a question.

"Does this mean we're not gonna fight?" inquired the brave known as Bag of Hammers.

NEW ORDER

"So you came for a visit," Watts Barber said from behind bars in the Southern Desert Correctional Facility back in Nevada. "How nice."

"Spare us," Camille Dishinstaller countered. "We just want you to know that we have no interest in pressing any charges against you."

"Wow, Dishy, I bet that's as close as you come to loyalty," the former dictator retorted. "If it wasn't for me, you'd be the toughest high school principal in Grand Island, Nebraska."

"And if it wasn't for me, Wattsy, where would you be?" inquired President Emelem Cox-Arquette, who was standing next to Dishinstaller, outside Barber's cell.

"Yeah, Uncle, there is that," Barber conceded. "But setting yourself up as president? Man, that's low-down."

"Between you, me and Dishy, I'm just holding onto the job as a negotiating chip. Not really feeling it, if you know what I mean."

"No," Barber said, seething with jealousy. "No, I don't. I can't believe how stupid I was to trust you two. Now I don't believe how stupid you're being."

"What do you mean?" Dishinstaller demanded.

"They're not going anywhere," Barber said, with eerie

calm. "The space monkeys are here to stay. They may let you have a title and a nice plush office but, you'll never be rid of them. Allies against the Terrahists! What were you thinking?"

What could she tell him? That the entire operation was payback for the lost training camp in Yosemite? That wouldn't even have been true. It all came down to one of her enemies and one of her officers uniting to rescue a damsel in distress. Noble? Sure. Romantic? Absolutely. Good statecraft? What would a Machiavellian like Watts Barber have to say about that?

She needn't have worried about Barber's opinion, of course, considering the invasion itself was rooted in personal motivations.

"The reason we came here," Dishinstaller explained, "was to let you know we'll be turning you over to Domestic justice. In exchange for being able to put you on public trial and broadcast it on DGN, the Domestic government has agreed to withdraw all forces, except for those technical advisors we ask for, to help us deal with the continued Terrahist threat."

"Sounds like a deal," Barber said. "'DGN'?"

"Daytrader Galacticam Network and, yes, it's a done deal. Goodbye, Mister President."

They turned and left, doing their best to ignore their former president yelling after them, "And you think you got a truce with the Terrahists? Don't mean nothin'! The second they see a percentage in it, they'll be openin' up another can of whoop-ass on you! You best listen to me! You best listen ..."

The cacophony of echoes obscured anything else Watts Barber had to say.

☆☆☆

The look he gave her through the prison bars continued to haunt Camille Dishinstaller. All through the insurgency, she had considered herself an American: free, independent and destined to win in the end. But seeing the man who had placed the Militia in her care, now a bedraggled hobo in a Las Vegas jail cell, sent the message straight through to the most primitive part of her brain: America was occupied. America lost. There was no more America.

Yes, there was a deal in place for the Domestic military to withdraw. But what was that deal worth? As far as she could tell, the Domestic headcount hadn't gone down by a single soldier and Sajak Pickfour, fresh from his landslide victory, felt no incentive to rush the process. And with Terrahists and rogue elements of the former insurgency continuing to snipe at Domestic troops, he still could claim provocation.

Early the next morning, it was with the slow deliberation of the vanquished that she shuffled from the Domestic-provided quarters at the Winn, down the Strip to the Bellagio, in response to a summons from Sanmateo Veecey.

She had to wait a short while in his outer office. She found it mildly amusing that the staffers who were coming and going were following orders written on their own arms.

After a few minutes, she was called in. There was music from another time playing on a Technics turntable. Dishinstaller, renaissance woman that she was, recognized it as the Beatles' *Abbey Road*. At that moment, the turntable was scratching out a movement known as 'I Want You (She's So Heavy).'

Veecey offered her a seat and she took it. He finished putting some lovingly-preserved vinyl records in a polymer packing crate, then took his own seat in front of the penthouse-level picture window. The first rays of dawn poked over the desert. As pretentious as she knew it looked, she found it necessary to put on her sunglasses indoors.

"Dishinstaller, we're at the end of a hard road."

"Speak for yourself."

"No, I mean both of us," Veecey said. "All of us.

American and Domestic. That's not to say we're not intersecting with some other hard roads."

"What's your point?"

The sun was growing more intense every moment. It was hard for Dishinstaller to see even with her shades on.

"My point is just this. America hasn't had a functioning government since all this began. It hasn't had a representational one in ages. If your nation is going to survive, it needs the right leader."

"What it needs is an end to occupation," she countered. "You people get back in your aluminum cans and go back where you come from and we'll worry about what kind of leaders we want."

"My government has authorized me to appoint an interim leader."

"When I kick you guys out past the Oort cloud, I'll have earned the right to be called America's leader."

"Well, that's just the thing. I can't imagine any way we can leave, without putting someone in place to fill the power void."

"Why not let Barber out?"

"You know President Pickfour has plans for him."

"Cox-Arquette?"

"He quit last night."

"He mentioned something about that to me. I didn't take him seriously."

"It's true. He cut a side deal with my boss, Admiral Daytrader."

"What's he getting?"

"California, south of Route 101 and west of 15," Veecey responded, as he flipped *Abbey Road* over and the room was filled with George Harrison's masterful chords opening side two, 'All the rest of America could be yours.'

By this time, the sun had risen high enough that it didn't appear to be focusing all its energy through that one window. Dishinstaller stood up. The view all at once struck her as a thing of beauty. She took off her sunglasses.

"I'll think about it," she said, in a tone of voice that could only mean 'yes.'

"Don't take too long," he said. "The sooner you agree, the sooner I get to quit."

He continued to pack his albums.

"Going back?" she asked.

"I've got nothing to go back to," Veecey replied after a pause. "Thought I'd wander around here a little, get to see what the rest of the planet is like."

☆☆☆

Sanjay Sanchez's funeral was a quiet, dignified affair to remember a quiet, dignified man.

As a favor to General Camille Dishinstaller, retired Sanmateo Veecey agreed to attend the funeral, although he declined to represent the Eminent Domain – or anybody but himself. As a further favor to Dishinstaller, he agreed to say a few words at the service, considering that Sanchez had very little family left and that none of his closest colleagues felt qualified to take on the obligation. So Veecey muttered a few aphorisms about duty, honor and how he respected this adversary-turned-ally, who shared this code. The remarks were perfectly appropriate and instantly forgettable.

As a final favor to Sanchez's commander, Veecey played a dirge at the graveside service. A bagpipe solo, she informed him, was required at all American funerals. He had never seen a bagpipe before that day and was surprised, early that morning, to find one had been delivered to the room he still had – until the end of the week – at the Bellagio.

When the bagpipe arrived, Veecey was unsure how to play it, or even how to tune it, or even if it could be tuned. He experimented a little and called it practice.

Veecey got dressed, went to the memorial chapel for the funeral, then followed the procession to the graveyard. As

Sanchez's coffin was lowered into the ground, Veecey improvised a mournful tune.

Bagpipes are a notoriously difficult instrument to master. It took adepts years of practice to be considered by those knowledgeable in bagpipes, even marginally qualified, to play in public. Someone, however gifted, who took one out of the box for the first time that morning would be dismissed straightaway as a poseur.

At Sanjay Sanchez's funeral, just as on most occasions at which the bagpipes were played, nobody could tell the difference.

There was a small reception back at the Winn, where many members of the American leadership were staying until the Domestic troops could fully withdraw from the Bellagio.

Veecey had stayed at the reception the requisite twenty minutes, had a cup of punch and was heading toward the door, when a dark, mysterious woman intercepted him.

"Thank you," she said by way of introduction.

"For what?" he asked. She had a familiar, not unattractive, face that he had been noticing on occasion all day, but was too distracted by his duties to pursue. She was also several years – many years – older than Iman Appdev.

"For your kind words about my big brother; for your music," she said. "I'm Selena."

"Mat. Mat Veecey."

"I know who you are. I just didn't know you were a musician."

"More like a music historian, but I play a couple of instruments."

"Not enough people play bagpipes anymore," she replied. "Considering all the funerals we've had here in America these past few years, we could have used a few more."

Veecey, not wanting to deal at that moment with the degree to which he'd contributed to the body count, thanked her for listening, excused himself, and pursued the door again. She blocked him again.

"Sorry," she said. "I don't know why I said that. It didn't come out the way I meant it."

"It's OK," he said.

"After all, you can't go back and undo anything. You don't accomplish anything by ..."

She was interrupted by a pubescent boy who shared her round face, high cheekbones and light-brown skin. He wanted her to give him money for something. Veecey really wasn't paying attention. The boy left as soon as Selena folded a couple of bills in his hand.

"That was my son, Santosh. Anyway, Mat, we can't look back. It's not fair to the children."

"I just don't want kids like your Santosh to have to go through that again," Veecey said, intended as an exit line.

"*Tienes razon.*"

Selena realized she had slipped up. Since the dawn of space travel, every school child knew humanity had moved toward standardization in language, to ensure that all people everywhere could communicate effectively. Using non-conforming patterns of speech in public was considered, by law, to be a crime against humanity. At a smaller, private gathering like the funeral reception, it was merely considered rude. But to Veecey, always with an ear for something new, it was a strange and enthralling surprise, not unlike the bagpipe. He found he was no longer in a rush for the exit.

"I mean, you're right."

Curiosity got the better of Sanmateo Veecey.

"But that's not what you said," he replied. "What was that?"

"It was my native language. Our family is not from America. We speak a non-standard dialect. It's called Mexican."

"I didn't know your brother was Mexican."

"He's not. He wasn't. We're not. The language is called

Mexican. We're Puerto Rican."

"Puerto Rican?" Veecey inquired, wrapping his mouth as best he could around the unfamiliar words. "I've never heard of that."

"There are very few of us left," Selena said. "In fact, now that Sanjay is gone, I don't know of any other Puerto Ricans, except for Santosh and me."

"Where did Puerto Ricans come from?" Veecey asked.

He expected her to come up with some glib, phony and obvious retort like 'Puerto Rico' or something similar to that.

But that's not what she said.

"New York," she said. "According to family lore, we live there still."

☆☆☆

"'Knees By Her Tits?'" General Camille Dishinstaller asked the younger woman, whom she had summoned to her office at the Winn.

"That wasn't the worst part, Ma'am," the once and current Iman Appdev responded. "I figured after a couple of kids, they'd be calling me 'Tits By Her Knees'."

Appdev, though on leave and dressed in civilian clothes, stood at full attention in the general's presence until Dishinstaller motioned to a chair, where Appdev settled, graceful as ever.

It was the first day since the insurgency began that Dishinstaller had worn her class-A uniform.

"Well, now that this is all over, Captain, what are you going to do with your life?" The last time Dishinstaller had seen Iman Appdev, the Domestic officer wore the buckskins of a Sioux maiden. She had updated her wardrobe since then but still seemed to favor short leather skirts. At any rate, it was apparent Appdev wasn't wearing her uniform unless she was compelled to do so.

"Haven't thought it all through, Ma'am," Iman Appdev

replied, rising to attention in front of Dishinstaller's desk. She marveled at how commanding Dishinstaller looked in comparison with the affable, but feckless, Sanmateo Veecey. "I imagine I'll return to PotteryBarnWorld – push all the adventures I've had and personal growth I've attained back to the darkest corners of my soul, marry a boy I thought was cute in school, have four children by him, work a minimum-wage job in the evening to supplement his seasonal, semi-skilled tradesman earnings and live a lower-middle-class existence until I die alone, a widow of twenty years."

"Maybe you'd accept another offer," said Dishinstaller, intuiting why Appdev was still single.

"Maybe," Iman Appdev replied, "but it would have to cut through generations of conditioning, selective breeding and social inertia."

"Well, I don't know what I can provide to compete with all that, but as you may know I recently lost my aide-de-camp. He was a very brave and capable man; he was a great loss to me personally, as well as professionally. I wouldn't ask just anyone to replace him."

"But you're asking me, Ma'am?"

"Yes, Captain."

"I can consider it only once my discharge from the Domestic military becomes final."

"Of course."

"And I would be uncomfortable swearing allegiance to another government. I'd have to serve in a non-uniformed capacity."

"I could live with that. We'll draw up papers making you a contractor."

"And I'd have to have my duties spelled out in some letter of agreement."

"No problem. It'll all be in those papers. In the meantime, I can tell you your duties would be similar to those you performed for General Veecey."

"Um, including those I performed only once?" Appdev asked.

"What? No. No!" General Dishinstaller said, with a how-dare-you undertone as she peered over her sunglasses. "Of course not. Pshaw!"

☆☆☆

In a bit of pointless, impotent, election-year hardball, the Loyal Opposition had held up Sajak Pickfour's nominees to fill the vacant posts of his depleted Steering Committee. It was just he and Admiral Reit Daytrader sitting at the conference table, while an enlarged array of functionaries swarmed behind them.

"Mister President, we simply can't afford to field an occupation force this large anymore," the galaxy's highest ranking military accountant said.

"So what are you suggesting?" the president asked. "We can't give up now. If we did, then all those fine Domestic soldiers who sacrificed their lives will have done so in vain. We must send more troops, so that when the ones who are there now are killed, they too shall be avenged. And we must keep sending troops to America, however many it takes, for as long as it takes, until they stop dying when we send them there."

"I'm not saying we should give up, Sir," Daytrader replied.

"What then?"

"Sub-contract it out."

"You mean pay someone else to die for us?"

"Uh, OK. Sir."

"Who would you recommend?"

"The Americans themselves," Daytrader explained. "We know they're good fighters, they know the terrain ... and we wouldn't have to pay travel, which saves about fifteen percent right there."

"Good thinking, Reitso. Get right on it."

"Yes Sir. One detail needs to be taken care of first."

"Go on."

"We're still fighting them."

"I'm guessing you have a solution to that, too."

"Yes, I do."

"Well, so do I," the president said, his chest puffing out. "We declare victory."

He expected Admiral Daytrader to respond 'Brilliant Sir' or at the very least, 'That's exactly what I was going to say.' But that's not what happened.

"We can't declare victory, Sir," Admiral Reit Daytrader explained.

"Well, why not?"

"First of all, we haven't won. Second of all, I don't think we ever actually, formally, officially, declared war, so I don't think we can declare victory."

"Well, I suppose you have a point."

"Thank you Sir," the president's last remaining top advisor said. "Um ... which one?"

"Well, winning and not winning are just a ..." the president consulted his word-a-day calendar here, "a *semantic* difference. But you're right, we can't call what we got now, a victory. So what else can we declare it?"

"A draw? A stalemate?"

"Reitso, I didn't ask what it is. I asked what we should call it."

"Adequate? Satisfactory?"

"Now you're talking."

"My friends," President Sajak Pickfour said to the live galacticam audience, addressing them from the grandest office in his mansion. "I come today to bring you news: delightful, adequate news. We have come to the long-awaited end of our passing interest in America. We have achieved much in our time here; the results of those achievements have been nothing short of satisfactory."

He paused for effect.

"And that means, things are OK. Back to normal. As well as can be expected. So we have upgraded our mission status to 'Satisfactory' from 'So Far, So Good.' And that means, in plain language, that our loyal and steadfast troops can disengage from their bases on Earth, so they can do what I know in their hearts they've wanted to do for a very long time: Go fight another war somewhere else."

"Forward posts will be withdrawn immediately and billeted in Las Vegas, then removed to transport craft in orbit, in an orderly order. Troops in high-risk areas like Palm Springs or Hollywood will cease patrols and take a defensive posture until the other troops have been processed out. In conclusion, the divisions based here in Las Vegas will vacate their positions according to a timetable to be negotiated with the newly-invested American government."

Immediately after the speech, Camille Dishinstaller contacted Sajak Pickfour. The negotiations went like this:

"You got thirty days."

"Camille, it's a complicated exercise. First we gotta ..."

"Not one second longer, Sajak."

"But ..."

"Time's wasting."

"But ..."

"Thirty."

"Oh, fine."

☆☆☆

In the same office from which he issued the famed 'Satisfactory' speech, Sajak Pickfour addressed the vanquished enemy.

"So what am I going to do with you?" the president of the Eminent Domain asked the former president of America.

Watts Barber stood before Sajak Pickfour bathed, shaved and wearing a fresh set of clothes, so as not to offend the sensitivities of Sajak Pickfour's courtiers. He wore a smile on his face, as if he were playing a joke that was on everybody else.

Still, Barber's hands were bound in front of him – not much of a restraint, both men understood, but great for the galacticam.

The cameras were waiting in the lobby of Pickfour's mansion. This discussion was private in its entirety between the two men, save for a small presidential guard presence.

"Just like you've always done, Jak," Barber replied. "Let me go."

"After all you've done against me and my nation?" Pickfour asked.

"Like what?"

"Like ... like ... um ... well, what about When All Hell Broke Loose?"

"You knew about that before I did."

"And WTF?"

"One of these days I'll have to tell you where they were the whole time," Barber said, adding for the record, "not that I have the itsiest-bitsiest clue right now."

"What about your support for the Terrahists?"

"We're neighbors, not friends. Their dogs shit all over my lawn too."

"How about your wars of aggression against every country you share a border with?"

"Got nothing to do with you, Jak."

"But you're a ruthless, savage, vicious, homicidal maniac who cares about nothing except his own power. I can't let you just walk out on Domestic justice."

"Nope, but you can hand me over to American justice."

"I don't follow."

"Look, you don't have enough to prosecute me for

jaywalking up here," Barber explained. "You send me back down to Earth. Dishy gets to preside over a sideshow trial, she'll sentence me to life imprisonment at one of our secret, high-security penal colonies for political prisoners and that'll be the last anyone hears from me."

"Sounds like you're looking forward to it."

"Knew this day was coming, Jak. Built one on Catalina. Co-ed - and I had the entire chorus line from the Sands banished there right before the war."

"Fine, I'll have my staff make the arrangements on two conditions," Pickfour announced. "First, President Dishinstaller must agree."

"Ain't like she don't owe me a coupla favors. Meantime, I can earn my keep helping you and her, behind the scenes, to bust some Terrahist ass. Second?"

"Second, I can come visit."

"It'll be just like back at the dorm, Jak."

"Can't hardly wait, Wattso," the most powerful man in the galaxy said, reaching into a mini-fridge and cracking open a couple of beers.

ONE YEAR LATER

M. Griffin Croupier VII had sworn never to set foot on Earth again but he had to come back for this day. He had also sworn never to be in the same room as Sajak Pickfour. But everyone who was anyone in the entire galaxy was in that Las Vegas wedding chapel. Pickfour was there with his wife, who waved like an animatronic piece of molded polymer, which of course she was. Like a rare and valuable gem, the real Spice Pickfour was rarely put on display. Or at least, that was the story.

Croupier, seated in his tuxedo, stared with longing at the altar, where the one woman he had ever been with was about to be joined forever. To someone else.

Croupier further swore he wasn't going to cry. When his handkerchief was reduced to the consistency of a used coffee filter, he swore never to swear again.

He had known for some time that it was Sanmateo Veecey who had him sent back home. For a long time, Croupier resented that but was, on this day of days, ready to shake hands and forgive. He was here as much at Veecey's invitation as at Appdev's.

Veecey stood near Appdev in front of the clergyman. Croupier was surprised to see him dressed similarly to himself, in the plain black-and-white formal wear of the

Domestic gentleman. He expected Veecey to sport the full dress uniform that he, even in retirement, was entitled to wear.

A shudder went up Croupier's spine when Veecey said, 'I do.' His shoulders shook.

"Save it," said Watts Barber, in casual attire, sitting next to him and doing his best with bound wrists to poke Croupier in the ribs. "The preacher just asked, 'Who comes to give this woman away?'"

Barber awkwardly maneuvered his arms to lend Croupier his own hanky. Through dabbed eyes, Croupier saw the tall, confident form of Lieutenant Colonel G.Q. Celltower, displaying with pride the Well Regulated Militia's dress blues.

Soon, it was Celltower's turn to say 'I do.'

The Appalachian-drawled question before him, though, had been, 'Who carries the rings as tokens of the vows about to be spoken?'

Miss Iman Appdev, a civilian now, was still in secondary school the last time Camille Dishinstaller wore her dress uniform. But the American commander looked every inch the gallant warrior - golden epaulets atop her shoulders, the glint of her saber's handle emerging from its scabbard, the patent leather of her boots shining like twin black suns. The sound of shattering glass came from under one of those boots as President Emeritus Emelem Cox-Arquette cried out "*Mazel Tov!*" to complete the ancient Hollywood ritual he had insisted upon. He was, after all, paying.

The dashing officer then, without waiting for official sanction, kissed her bride.

All at once, Croupier wasn't the only one crying.

It was a traditional American wedding reception: overcooked chicken cordon bleu, Electric Slide, friendly cake fight between the brides, hostile fist fight between their families. M. Griffin Croupier caught the bouquet, elbowing out a petite but well-toned mocha-skinned woman, who was particularly aggressive in her pursuit of the prize. Croupier noticed that, at the end of the reception, she left with Sanmateo Veecey.

Earlier in the evening, though, Veecey had a brief but poignant dance with his long-time unrequited love.

"I wish you happiness and ..." he choked on the word, "... love."

"I wish you the same, Mat."

"You sure this is what you want? I don't just mean Camille. I mean Earth. America."

"I found a home here," she said meekly.

"Guess I'm still looking."

They held each other for a few moments in silence.

"Iman?"

"Hmm?"

"Do me a favor."

"Sure."

"Never forget where you come from. Never forget you were once a soldier of the Eminent Domain."

She gripped him in a tight embrace.

"Oh, Mat, if we have a baby," she said, all at once wistful, "we'll name it 'Shmuck'."

Pickfour danced with his wifebot, passing close to where Watts Barber had two bound hands around the neck of his successor, Camille Dishinstaller. Over their partners' shoulders, Barber mouthed to Pickfour, 'Meet me later,' gave him a lecherous frat-boy wink, then shot his eyes on the back exit.

At the end of the reception, one of the brides decorously went over to thank the officiator of the ceremony.

"Great job, Rev," Iman A. Dishinstaller said, giving the clergyman a peck on his mutton-chopped cheek, the white tide of satin that formed the tail of her gown whipping around the rhinestones on his jumpsuit.

"Thankyuh," the cleric replied. "Thankyuhvurimuch."

POSTSCRIPT

Dear Reader,
   Everything in the book you just read was a joke.
   Except the title.

Author

Rebel Publishers
we publish good books

We hope you enjoyed *Land That I Love.* by William Freedman.
Please turn the page for a preview of his upcoming novel,
Mighty Mighty.

MIGHTY
MIGHTY

WILLIAM FREEDMAN

PROLOGUE

*B*OOM! POW! A sharp left and a sharper right made quick work of the last two henchmen as Colonel America charged at the villainess. Mainan Brigitte had dared to take hostage the Colonel's comrades, The Crusaders (the crusaders!!!), and he was the only one left to charge to the rescue.

Aside from the Colonel, his teammates, Brigitte and her Institute minions, Park Avenue stood abandoned from 34th Street to Central Park South. Even the NYPD had been cleared out by National Guard troops who secured the famed, flower-basketed boulevard. Outside, the Manhattan air sat muggy and unseasonably warm in the pre-dawn. The Colonel was finding it hard to breathe, though he had the battle almost won.

The only thing that stood between Colonel America and his adversary was a glass counter; the entranceway into Tiffany's having been demolished in the early-morning donnybrook. The battleground that the previous day had been a shop of rare and unique objects of wonder was now a common shambles. Individually and in packs, the eldritch artifacts littered the store. Over here: cards that could conjure the strength of mighty athletes, long departed but still summonable to play their positions. Over there: cards that gave form to pocket-monsters or digital-monsters, so that their possessors could duel for supremacy. Behind the glass counter, Maman Brigitte intended to leave all these valuable talismans behind to escape with the rarest card of them all.

"The gig is up, Maman Brigitte!" Colonel America shouted. "Surrender ... or else!"

Maman was a ghostly figure, dressed in a diaphanous black shroud and matching headscarf. Her face, black as a moonless midnight, was as hollow and austere as her figure was tall and lithe. She confronted her adversary who was clad in primary-colored body armor and cowl, folded-over boots and famous bulletproof flag-cape.

"I think that's 'jig,'" she corrected in her thick Creole accent. "'The jig is up.'"

"Really? Are you sure?" the Colonel paused, perplexed. "I've been saying 'gig' all this time."

Suspended three feet off the floor in a cage composed of black magicks and white bones ripped from the security guards, the other four members of the Colonel's team shook their heads or rolled their eyes. The big one, made of soft, black, crumbly sediment spoke for them all. "Colonel!" the Carbon Avenger shouted. "Remember what we told you about banter!"

"Sorry, Avenger!" Colonel America said to his teammate while Maman Brigitte smashed open the glass counter and pulled out an ornate, two-by-four-inch tin with xxmalificiumxx engraved across it in gothic letters, the u carved like a v.

The colonel droned on, "Remember, even the best of us still has a couple areas he'd like to improve ..."

"Shut up and subdue her already!" the Carbon Avenger advised.

But just as the Colonel was vaulting over the counter and ready to put a gloved hand across her throat, he was overcome with the fumes of a thousand Haitian fire peppers.

His eyes burned like a deep breath of ammonia. In a puff of putrid smoke, Maman Brigitte was gone. Her voice lingered on for a moment, "Now I need but one more ..." then degenerated into a fading cackle.

As the voodoo priestess's presence receded, the cage that held her captives disintegrated. All but insect-sized Midge, who had wings, fell to the floor. Pantagruel, the World's Largest Human, hit particularly hard, flat on his coccyx. Midge, his wife, tittered at this until Pantagruel shot her a killing look.

"She's got almost the entire deck," the Carbon Avenger exposited. "We've got to find that last Malificium card before she does or the world is doomed!"

"Wherever it is," Colonel America pondered, "Let's hope that it's protected by guardians worthy of their fateful role."

"For now, though, we should get back to the Pinnacle and see if we can figure out where this rarest of all Malificium cards is," the Carbon Avenger suggested. "As for who might currently be charged with its safekeeping, we just have to leave that to a higher power."

The Colonel, Midge, and Pantagruel all nodded in agreement. The fifth member of their cohort merely smiled his beneficent smile.

ABOUT THE AUTHOR

William Freedman is a New York-based satirist who uses science fiction and fantasy tropes. He is author of *Mighty Mighty* and *Land That I Love*, co-author with Ben Parris of *Supernaturalz*, contributor to the 2005 Spirit House chapbook to raise money for tsunami survivors, and a frequent program participant at genre conventions throughout the northeast U.S.

Most recently, he served as editor for the *Age of Certainty: What if God Existed?* anthology. His non-fiction bylines – covering everything from hot stocks for Investor's Business Daily to the rise of distilled spirits for History magazine to Bram Stoker Awards weekend for Long Island's Newsday – go back more than 20 years.